# Rita Wong and the Jade Mask

# Rita Wong and the Jade Mask

## Mark Jones

Published in the UK by Everything with Words Limited
Fifth Floor, 30–31 Furnival Street, London EC4A 1JQ

www.everythingwithwords.com

A catalogue record of this book is available
from the British Library.

ISBN 978-1-911427-18-6

Printed and bound in Great Britain by
CPI Group (UK) Ltd, Croydon CR0 4YY

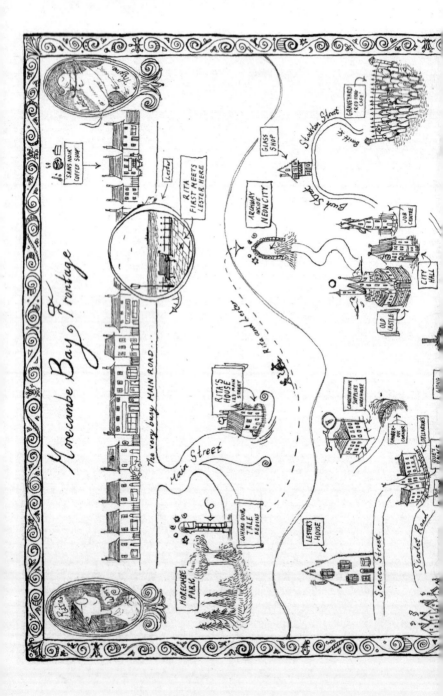

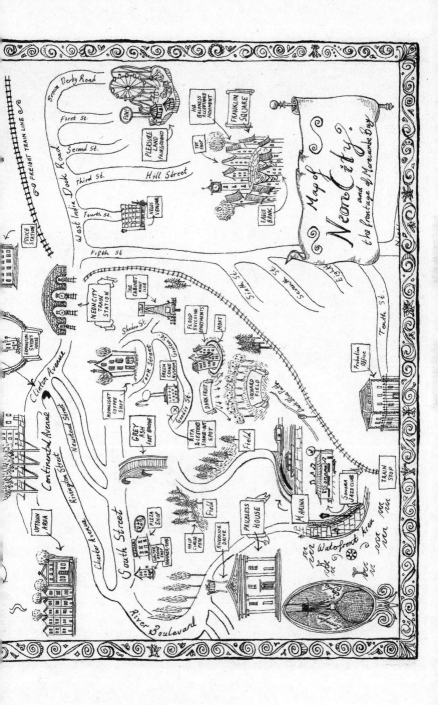

Map of
*Neon City*
and
the frontage of Norcombe Bay

# CHAPTER ONE

## A Bad Night at the Toy Shop

A small lithe man in a big top hat was carrying an enormous sheet of copper. He looked over his shoulder and opened the door to a toy shop. Inside the shop was warm and carried the scent of orange chocolate. Looking around, the man spotted a shelf containing an arrangement of dusty figures. He smiled at a vampire doll in a white bridal gown but frowned at the sight of a toy tiger with black stripes and brown eyes.

Adjusting his top hat, the man turned and made his way to the back of the shop. There he descended a staircase that led to a basement. He stepped through a pair of black silk curtains at the bottom of the stairs. A clock in the basement chimed thirteen but no one was counting.

'Is this the headquarters of the *Baldness Acceptance Movement?*' the man asked.

A friendly balding werewolf stood up. He had been seated behind a circular walnut table that took up half of the basement and was littered with sweet wrappers.

'It certainly is,' answered the werewolf. 'And we're always happy to have new members.'

The man bowed deeply, hiding his face with the brim of his hat. He dropped the sheet of copper he had been carrying to the floor. A loud clang passed through the room. He removed his top hat to reveal a glossy, brown, full head of hair. His young striking profile was defined by an emerald spotlight. His eyes looked at the occupants of the basement, while his mouth stretched into a smile.

'My, my,' he said. 'I always wondered what a room full of giant hard-boiled eggs would look like.'

A nine-foot troll stood up from behind the table. The eyes in his face bulged more than his muscles.

'Buddy, I don't think I like your sense of humour,' he said.

'Sorry,' the man in the top hat replied. 'I've survived a dangerous night, and I just wanted a chuckle. I'm just practising being social. But don't you worry. I'll be *hair* today and gone tomorrow,' he said, before leaning forward and letting out a laugh.

'Another wisecrack like that, and you'll be sorry,' the werewolf announced, his hands balling into fists.

The man in the top hat smiled and approached the table. He walked briskly across a black and white marble floor.

'If you try and make me sorry,' he whispered, 'I'll polish your head like a filthy window. You have a temper like a tiger snake, my friend. But my bite is more lethal than yours. Now you and your friends should take a seat while I explain why I'm here.'

The troll picked up the table and threw it across the room. The impact ripped a yellow pipe from the wall which began to hiss steam. Above, a red strobe light began to blink.

'I think it's time for you to leave,' said the troll.

'How are you going to make me, Mr Shampoo Dodger?'

The troll charged across the room. He grunted and snorted as he lowered his head to attack.

The man in the top hat neatly sidestepped out of the way. Instead of meeting his opponent head-on, the man threw a volley of quick punches into the troll's back. He followed them up with an arm twist and a powerful back kick.

The troll was lifted cleanly off his feet. He felt himself fly across the room, and land back on his chair. The expression on his face was one of surprise and fear.

'My name is Ermington Snyde,' the man in the top hat announced. He squatted down on the floor to pick up the metal sheet. He removed a hammer from his pocket and nailed the copper layer to a wall. An atmosphere of evil then entered the room, and he left the occupants of the basement to endure it.

Glancing out of the toy shop's front window, Ermington heard a crack of thunder and watched the heavens open. The pavement, now slick with a deluge of rain, reflected a harmony of colours coming from neon lights in the street. As he stepped into the mist saturated night, he turned to face the front door.

Turning the key in the Chubb lock twice,

Ermington smiled to himself. The second rotation pushed the deadbolt further into the jamb. No one would be entering or leaving the toy shop ever again. He then snapped the key between his fingers, before disappearing into the jagged carbon black shadows of Neon City.

# CHAPTER TWO

## A Few Days Earlier in a Lonely Place

Tillotama Kumar had met a lot of serious children and teenagers in her time. None, however, were quite as serious as Rita Wong.

For the last hour in the coffee shop, Rita had never looked up. She had buried her head in a book about Art Deco, stopping only to sketch in her notepad.

'Hey, bookworm, you want another hot chocolate?'

'Well,' said Rita checking her mobile phone. 'The library doesn't open until nine o'clock. So, sure. I'd like another please, Miss Kumar.'

'Please call me Tilo. Saying "Miss Kumar" all the time reminds me I'm thirty-five.'

'Sorry, Tilo.'

'You know, you're far too efficient for this town.'

'How so?'

Tilo put a heavy coffee pot on the cherry-wood table between them. She took a seat and ran a hand through her dusky braided hair.

'This is Morecambe. English coastal towns are not like big cities. We do everything slow here. Relaxing with good food and drink is more important than being clockwise.'

'I just want to practise my drawing,' Rita replied, putting her book away.

'Ah, I see. You want to be a better artist than your father? That will take some doing. I hear he's a master with charcoal.'

'Oh, he is good,' Rita agreed. 'But I prefer Biro pens. They make nice clean lines.'

Tilo folded her arms across her chest. 'Morecambe is full of clean lines. And they will still be there tomorrow. But today is a Saturday. Are you sure you want to spend it alone in the library?'

'My father was going to take me to the movies. But he had to leave early this morning. Something about a bridge in Sunderland.'

'That's too bad,' Tilo said, her large brown eyes full of sympathy. 'He's a busy engineer, so there's not much he can do about it. Is his boss still making him drive all over England?' she asked, her small figure framed by a wall of jade-green tiles.

'Yes, he's busier than ever.'

'The library it is then I suppose. But maybe while you're there, can you do me a favour?'

'Of course,' Rita replied, her curiosity aroused.

'Good. But first I'll get that hot chocolate, then I'll tell you about the favour.' Tilo picked up the silver coffee pot and sauntered over to a rosewood counter. As she put the pot down, an espresso machine hissed at her like a resentful cobra.

Rita looked at the sunlight pouring in to the coffee shop. It divided neatly between the Venetian blinds, illuminating chrome, wood, and ceramics. Speakers in the ceiling above her poured out jazz music. The silky beats drifted through the air, relieving tension.

'Here's your assignment,' said Tilo, appearing from behind Rita. She briefly touched the tip of her nose as she sat down. 'I want you to draw this for me.' She placed a small blue striped box in front of Rita.

Inside the box was a gold ring in the shape of

a coiled snake. Set into the top of the ring was an emerald.

'Oh! That's so cool. Where did you get it, Tilo?'

'Someone I once loved gave it to me.'

'I like the snake,' said Rita, her green eyes lighting up in excitement.

'I thought you would. You like creepy stuff don't you?'

'Snakes aren't creepy.'

'Wait till a great big one bites you. Then you'll change your mind. Now,' Tilo gently placed the ring on Rita's index finger. 'Take good care of it. And bring it back only once you've drawn it. I'd better get back and fix that espresso machine. Who knows what else will break down today?'

Rita held her new ring up to the light and ran a finger across the emerald. The smooth gemstone had some kind of character engraved onto its surface. The marking was composed of thirty strokes. Rita did not know what the character meant, but somehow it seemed familiar.

Rita caught a glimpse of something across the road as she finished her hot chocolate. It was someone, or something, about eight feet in height.

'It' had decided to be brave, and was walking along Morecambe Bay in the numbing cold. It moved sturdily against the icy wind. Then it stopped to remove a hat from its head. It waved the hat in the air to shake the snow away.

Rita stood up and walked closer to the coffee shop's front window. She could now see that the thing had a large bald head. That would be nothing out of the ordinary. However, the head was not only large and bald but also green in colour.

Rita buttoned up her coat, picked up her backpack and stepped through the front door of the coffee shop. Her curiosity had overridden her caution. Outside, an ice-cold wind brushed against Rita's cheek and kept going. It saw no reason to stay.

Tilo watched Rita leave the warmth of the *Sans Noir* coffee shop. Her eyes tracked the movements of the teenage girl who was now putting on a pair of winter gloves.

As Tilo returned to repair her espresso machine, a mischievous smile danced across her face. 'Well, Ms Wong, I wonder if I'll ever see you again?' she said, under her breath.

# CHAPTER THREE

## Snow Passage

Rita removed a tartan beret from her coat pocket and wiped her round spectacles. It was still bitterly cold even though the snow had stopped falling. The chilly air stung her nostrils as she crossed the road, and the wind howled in her ears.

The bayfront was encased in pure white snow. A small bench was icily dressed with a winter's topping and comfortable only for a snowman. By the side of it, the mysterious green-headed figure had come to a stop. It was staring out at the waters of the bay and across to the Lakeland Fells as if lost in thought. Rita noticed it had a wide green tail with several sharp spikes. Neatly folded on its back were a pair of wings. The figure was wearing white socks, white trainers, and a pair of grey tracksuit bottoms.

Rita could not help giggling at the tracksuit bottoms. She was soon heard by their owner who turned around.

'What are you laughing at, shorty?' they asked in a posh voice.

Rita looked up at a face that was green and hard like poplar wood. There were several sharp-edged teeth set in a wide sulking mouth. Above the mouth, a pair of immense eyes that looked both sad and hopeless. They were tortoiseshell brown in colour. The ears were small and stuck out. The head was crowned by an old black beanie hat stretched across it.

'Yes, keep laughing,' said the figure. 'I'll stand here all day if it helps.'

'I'm sorry,' Rita replied, trying to catch her breath after chuckling. 'It's good to see someone dressed up for fun. Are you meant to be a dragon?'

'My word, you're quick. You must be a detective?'

'No, I'm still at school,' replied Rita. 'Say, aren't you a bit small for a dragon?'

The dragon took a sharp breath. He then held up a claw as if making an important announcement.

'Listen, imps who live in glass houses shouldn't throw stones. Now, why don't you and your attitude problem, take a walk.'

'You're the one with the attitude problem. I hope you enjoy the party. It must be a special one, for people with no sense of humour!'

'Party? What party would that be?'

'The fancy dress party you're going to.'

'Listen, young lady. Making fun of someone's clothes is a hate crime.'

'No, I meant—'

'I know exactly what you meant,' the dragon replied, nodding his head and sounding hurt. He thrust his hands into his tracksuit pockets, and his breath became visible in the cold air. 'Just because you're rolling in cash doesn't give you the right to judge me. So don't play me for a fool,' he added, raising his chin.

'Don't you make enough money from your job?'

The dragon went silent. When he spoke again it was in a whisper: 'At the moment I don't work.'

'You mean you're unemployed?'

15

'Quiet!' shrieked the dragon glancing around as if the police were looking for him. 'I am trying to find a job.'

'Sorry,' said Rita, realising she had touched a raw nerve. 'What's your name?'

The dragon looked down. 'My name is Lester Thyme,' he replied, smiling ever so slightly and nodding his head.

'Lester is it? My name is Rita. Can I ask, are you a real dragon?'

'Well of course I am!'

'Can you make your tail move to prove it?' she asked, rubbing her chin in curiosity.

Lester obliged and waved his tail in the air from left to right. He raised an eyebrow and winked. 'How do you like that?' he asked.

'That's impressive, but what are you doing here?'

'This place holds good memories for me. It reminds me of being younger and having lots of friends. Now I'm on my own all the time.'

'I can relate to that,' Rita replied. She then went on to tell him about all the friends she had left behind in Hong Kong, but she kept her feelings of homesickness to herself.

'And you've only been here for two months? That's a lot to happen in a short time.'

'Yes, I suppose,' said Rita , feeling better for having told someone.

'How old are you?'

'I'm thirteen years old, but I'll be fourteen in a week,' she said, stamping her feet to try and keep warm.

'You have your whole life ahead of you,' said Lester, looking slightly jealous. 'But never take time for granted. If only I could—' An orange watch on his wrist beeped abruptly. A look of panic spread across Lester's face. 'I'll be late, they'll kill me!' he said in horror.

'Who's going to kill you?'

The dragon did not stick around to answer the question but set off running across the road. Rita ran after him, her boots trampling the snow. Her trouser legs became wet as she dashed through pools of cold water. Behind her, tyres crushed the rock salt on the road melting the ice away and car engines revved. Their exhaust fumes moved through the icy air.

Lester Thyme first raced down the broad pavement of Main Street. Then he made a right onto Vine

Street which was lined with hawthorn trees. Twice Rita shouted for him to stop, but Lester's bulky figure continued to charge down the street like an elephant. He was heading towards a small park. It had a wooden entrance arch decorated in red Chinese writing. One of the characters on the arch was composed of thirty strokes.

'Wait!' Rita shouted. She was close to the dragon and closing in. Her pace accelerated and cut through the cold wind. On her left, a workman watched her pass as his jackhammer broke through the pavement at his feet. The pneumatic banging was unnoticed by Rita, who was on the coat-tails of the dragon. She was neck and neck with him as they passed through the arch. Then there was a flash of blue light and a loud crack of thunder.

# CHAPTER FOUR

## Detour

Rita stopped dead in her tracks. Sunlight and snow had disappeared. Around her, she could feel the embrace of a hot tropical night. There was a smell of smoke in the air with a taste of charcoal. In front of her hung a cluster of tall buildings. They were layered with neon signs in a dazzling array of blues, purples, reds, and yellows. They contained logograms which Rita could not understand. She scanned the cityscape for a sign she could read.

Rita looked around and hoped to see something familiar. The only thing she did recognise was Lester who was still running away from her. 'Please slow down!' she shouted, but he was too far away to hear. She tried to follow him and ran along a smooth tarmac pavement. There was a glow of light here and there as she passed under copper streetlights. A low hum of machinery drifted in the shadows. In the distance, a foghorn went off.

The dragon was running away in a zigzag pattern. He took a right here and a left there and kept on going like a mouse in a maze. As Rita rounded a corner, she felt sweaty and her breaths were desperate. Up ahead, she saw the dragon open a door and step off the pavement.

Slowing to a walk, Rita removed her coat and winter gloves. The building Lester had entered was an old grey brick castle. She leaned against the castle wall and tried to get her breath back. The bricks throbbed. As she snatched her hands back, blue light pulsed where her fingers had been. She had the feeling the building was purring like a happy cat who had just been stroked. The effect was soothing but mysterious.

Looking around, Rita felt slightly cautious. 'This street... what is this place?' she wondered. She decided she was lost and considered it safer to follow the dragon. He seemed honest enough, and he could shed some light on where she was.

In the far distance, a factory steam whistle hollered. Rita noticed there was no moon in the sky and no sign of life in the streets. There was nothing to reassure or guide her.

'Google Maps,' whispered Rita. She reached into her backpack and removed a small mobile phone. It clicked open but showed no signal. Google Maps did not respond. Then there was the clock on the front screen. The time display had frozen. Reluctantly, she put her phone away. She had the feeling she was being watched.

When Rita looked up, her legs began to shake. Between two of the castle's turrets was a walkway made of glass. A gigantic spider was looking down at her from the walkway. In the dim light, its red eyes glowed like teardrops of blood. Its mouth, a long hairy ridge, suddenly smiled. Rita noticed it was holding a mop between two of its legs. One of its other legs turned off a small radio, then waved as if encouraging her to enter the building.

In front of her was the aluminium entrance door which Lester had passed through. On the door, arranged in a line, were some curvy symbols that looked like writing.

Looking up at the spider, Rita gave him a thumbs-up sign. The spider nodded his head and continued his mopping.

Opening the door, Rita discovered a brightly lit lobby area with a polished silver floor. The walls around it were clad with dark oak and gave the impression the castle was a lavish hotel.

At the end of the lobby was an open door with a chrome-plated frame. Through the frame, she could see a wide corridor with red rose wallpaper. On the floor was a thick carpet with a geometrical design of pink and white.

Rita decided to follow the corridor. The air within it felt fresh but smelt slightly chemical. At the end of the corridor was a spiral staircase of narrow stone steps. As she reached the bottom of the staircase, she discovered another corridor. From above, she could hear what sounded like a wolf howling.

Coming to a stop, Rita paused and considered turning back. She decided the best idea was to keep moving forward. As she did so, the corridor became colder and narrower. The ceiling above was already low and becoming lower by the minute. The walls around her were slimy with some kind of green goo.

Rita felt isolated, disoriented and lost. She started to get a headache, and the lights above began to flicker. Feeling hemmed in, she decided to return to the lobby. After a short run, she could feel the floor beneath her vibrate.

As Rita changed direction, she noticed a black marble trap door on the floor. It was four feet in length. Although athletic, she was not confident of being able to jump clear of it. That was when the light went out. She was now alone in the dark. In front of her, she heard a creaking sound as if a door had opened. Shivering in the dark, she realised the trap door had opened.

'Now it's dark. And once you come in here, you can't walk out easily,' a thick gravelly voice said. It was coming from somewhere in the gloom.

Rita, feeling the cold bite into her, began to panic. She suddenly remembered her mother's advice about difficult situations: always take a moment and think about what to do next. She sat in a cross-legged position on the floor and took several deep breaths. Feeling calmer, she decided all she could do was talk to the voice.

'If you're going to make threats you should at least show yourself!' she said.

'Who's making threats?' the voice asked.

'You are,' Rita answered. 'You could have introduced yourself and told me who you are. Instead, you tell me I can't leave!'

'I did no such thing!'

'Yes, you did.'

'You misunderstand me,' the voice replied. 'I merely meant getting back to the front door isn't easy. And who are you?'

'My name is Rita.'

'Rita is it? And why, Miss Rita, did you come down here?'

'I'm looking for my friend.'

'Who's this friend of yours?'

'He's a dragon called Lester.'

'Nah, don't know him,' the voice said and went quiet.

'Are you going to just leave me here all alone in the dark?' Rita asked.

'And what do you want me to do about it?'

'Can you get me out of here or take me to someone who can help?'

'Well, I suppose I could. Would you like me to do that?'

'Of course, you idiot! I don't want to live in the dark for the rest of my life.'

'Alright, alright,' the voice said in defeat. 'Wait there. I'll come and take you to someone.'

A long silence followed. Rita was beginning to wonder if the voice was some kind of trickster. Eventually, she heard a harsh whisper coming from just over her shoulder.

'Are you ready?'

'Yes, but aren't you going to turn the light on?'

'I can't. The bulb's gone.'

'Can't you change it?'

'Not when there's austerity. But hold my hand and I'll lead you out of here.'

Rita stood up. She opened her left hand and it was taken by a cold clammy grip. Not ideal, but better than being in the dark forever. As they walked farther down the corridor, she noticed the air becoming warmer. Just ahead, she could see lit torches attached to the walls. The corridor had also become wider while the ceiling had receded.

She turned to thank whoever the voice was, but there was no one there. In her open palm, she could still feel the cold wet fish that was the voice's hand.

'Here you are,' the voice said. 'Now, just keep walking and there's a small door ahead. Walk through it and someone there will be able to give you directions.'

The voice let go of her hand, and his footsteps could be heard fading away in the background. Just ahead, as he had promised, was a small iron door with a rusty handle and a silver lock. Rita opened it and walked into the adjoining room. The small metal door closed behind her and locked itself.

The room, filled with hundreds of candles, was hauntingly radiant. It was windowless and the walls dripped with grey peeling paint. In the centre of the room was a long black wooden object held high by a latticework of twisted metals. Rita stepped closer and realised the object was a coffin.

A master of carpentry had obviously built the coffin. It was lacquered and of exquisite workmanship. The style appeared Transylvanian, and there were carved circles on the surface with spikes within them.

To Rita's dismay, the coffin started to tremble and convulse. Rising into the air, it then crashed to the ground with an almighty boom. It made one last discharge and then fell silent. From inside could be heard a series of clicking sounds and the coffin popped open.

Rita, frozen to the spot, saw that a young woman dressed in a black silk dress had risen from the coffin. In the candlelight, the woman's skin was like porcelain and had a reflective quality. Her lips were plump and red yet also delicate. Her forehead was small, perfectly round, and her long smooth nose gave her a regal look. Her face was set in a cute heart-shaped head with long glossy black hair.

'Seriously, the equipment they give me,' the woman said. 'I'm going to tell them at the next office meeting. How would they like to be... And who might you be?' she asked, in a soft honey-coated voice.

'My name is Rita and I'm lost.'

'Aren't we all, my dear? I left Korea a hundred years ago and wish I'd never bothered. My name is

Kim Park, and I'm an administrator. What can I do to help?'

'I'm looking for my friend. He's a dragon and his name is Lester. I followed him here but then I got lost. Can you help me?'

'I believe I could. Are you human?' Kim asked, looking Rita over.

'Yes.'

'Have you ever had your heart broken?'

'No, I—'

'Lucky you. Neither had I until I came here. I used to be fun and at peace with myself. Trust me. Never fall in love,' Kim said, the inner edges of her eyebrows rising together.

Rita smiled in an attempt to show she was paying close attention, but inside she felt depressed. It had begun the moment Kim Park had started to speak. A feeling of negativity passed through her and she felt drained.

'Then this job! Since they got rid of computers, we all have to work seven days a week. And all—'

'I hate to interrupt, but I don't have much time,' Rita said.

'I can go on a bit, can't I? Now this friend of yours,

let's see.' Kim pulled a small black book from inside her coffin. As she looked through it, she touched a fang in her upper jaw.

'Found him! He'll be on the third floor. I can take you there if you like?'

'That would be great if you could.'

'Right then, better hop on board,' Kim said, opening a flap in the coffin to reveal a red silk seat. 'Come on, don't be shy. I won't bite, I promise.'

Rita climbed on top of the coffin and wedged herself into the deep comfortable seat. Looking up, she noticed a circular brick hole in the ceiling. The coffin doubled as some kind of elevator. With a sound like steam being released, the coffin elevator took off.

# CHAPTER FIVE

## The Stranger on the Third Floor

The upper floor of the castle was modern, neat, but relatively threadbare. In each corner of the vast room was a square mahogany desk. There were no computers in sight and the place had the air of an old-fashioned government department.

The middle section of the room had been arranged as a waiting area. There were hundreds of chairs with all kinds of creatures sitting in them. Some had fallen asleep while others seemed on edge.

Overall, the room felt cold and smelt damp. It had a feeling of desperation, mixed with a fear of the future. It was lit with unnatural blue lighting but with neither light bulbs nor candles in sight.

Rita noticed something blurry travelling from one corner of the room to another. It appeared like a snowdrift and then transformed into a man. As she walked farther into the room, she caught a better look. The man had a rough grey beard, untidy grey hair, and two large imposing yellow eyes. He wore an ill-fitting red polyester shirt with a white tie. Within seconds, the man disappeared and reappeared at another desk.

'He looks like an angry Father Christmas,' Rita thought to herself.

Noticing an empty red and blue armchair, Rita decided to sit down and gather her thoughts. In a seat to her left, a small rotund dwarf was dressed in a denim jacket and jeans. He seemed to be looking through the sports pages of a newspaper. He had put too much aftershave on, and a strong smell of flowers assaulted her senses.

'Something wrong, miss?' the dwarf asked.

'Nothing at all,' Rita said, holding her breath and turning to face the other way. On her right was a werewolf dressed in office attire. He had a small diamond stud in his left ear. On top of his head was a huge comb-over haircut. Rita bit her tongue and tried not to laugh.

'Are you laughing at me because I'm going bald?' the werewolf asked, looking irritated.

'Who me? Absolutely not,' Rita said, covering her mouth with a hand.

'Everyone laughs,' the werewolf said, his eyes bulging. 'They think I don't know. But I know exactly what all of them are thinking.'

'Who are "they"?' Rita asked.

'Oh, you know. You've been in on it from the start!' the werewolf replied, his eyes a whirlpool of paranoia. 'But I will tell you this much,' he announced at the top of his voice. 'If one more person makes fun of me... why I'll—'

'Alright, enough of that. Give us a break, slaphead,' the Father Christmas look-alike grunted. He glanced at a piece of paper in his left hand. 'Lester Thyme, you are next!' he shouted.

Rita looked forward and saw Lester. He was strolling over to a chair in front of the grey-haired man's desk.

'Good morning, Warlock Devlin. How are you?' Lester asked, lowering his head.

'What have you been doing to find work in the last two weeks?' the warlock demanded.

Suddenly, Lester appeared to begin sweating. He also rubbed his neck and his top lip started to tremble.

'I've checked all the newspapers every day, sir, and—'

'Not good enough!' the warlock replied, his face first a sneer and then a smug grin.

Lester gulped and continued to explain: 'I've called lots of local firms on the telephone and—'

'Still not good enough. You have two weeks to find a job or you're off benefits!' Warlock Devlin shouted, slamming his right hand on the desk. 'I believe you also rent a council house, and the rent's past due?' The warlock looked Lester up and down. 'You'll soon be needing an extra-large cardboard box,' he added.

'I'll get a job, I promise,' Lester said.

'Good!' the warlock growled. He took a small cheque from his desk drawer, signed it, and threw it on the floor.

Lester bent down to put the cheque in his wallet.

As he did, he looked up at the warlock and smiled gently.

'Don't you have better things to be doing than eyeballing me?' the warlock asked, turning over a piece of paper he had been writing on. His lips stretched sideways revealing thick yellow teeth. 'Maybe you should pay more attention to your own affairs. That way you won't keep missing the obvious!'

Lester took a deep breath and lowered his voice until it became a whisper.

'Give all my love to Mrs Santa Claus.'

'What! What did you just say to me?'

'I said my job search must be flawed. I'll keep looking.'

The dragon then walked towards the castle's exit. Rita rose from her chair and followed him. Outside, he turned around to look at her. 'You shouldn't follow strangers. What are you doing here?'

'I was worried about you. And who was that man shouting at you?'

'He's no friend of mine, that's for sure.'

'You shouldn't have let him speak to you like that.'

'But I need all the yen I can get.'

'Yen?'

'It's money. You must know that if… wait a minute,' Lester said, pointing upwards. 'What does the sign at the front of the castle say?'

'I don't know how to read it,' Rita said, hunching her shoulders.

'It's a mix of languages. And it spells out the word *Jobcentre*. Are you saying you've never been here before?'

'I don't even know where we are.'

'Your parents must be doing well. Anyway, we're outside City Hall. You know what? I'm confused and a little tired. What do you say I buy you a drink?'

# CHAPTER SIX

## Blues in the Night

Rita was looking from side to side as she followed Lester. They had left the built-up section of the city and were passing through a residential area. The streets they followed seemed coated on both sides with the facades of small red-brick terraced houses.

The area around the houses looked quaint and comfortable. There were violet lilac trees positioned every few feet along the pavement. She could feel the ground quiver whenever an underground train flowed by.

Rita noticed that Lester was taking everything in

his stride. He seemed to know exactly where he was going. He obviously knew the place and must have spent a lot of time in it. It made her feel less helpless, but also dependent on a stranger.

The city was Lester's home and he walked slowly down Bush Street from City Hall. He then made a left onto Stockton Street and then a second right turn onto Burritt Street.

'We're here,' he said, pointing across the street.

Rita turned to look and saw a graveyard.

'What? Are you joking?'

The graveyard had small rolling drifts of green fog which moved towards them like waves on the shore. Sticking up here and there were weather-beaten gravestones inscribed in a multitude of languages. Three metres into the graveyard the fog was so thick it seemed to be blocking the path.

'Don't be put off,' Lester said. 'We're just going to a small cafe through here. The ghosts are even-tempered. They actually like company and, as it's midnight, it's now happy hour. You must be thirsty?'

'I don't think I'm that thirsty. You're convinced it's safe in there?'

'Trust me.'

'I'll take your word for it,' she said and followed him in.

They trudged through high grass which was both wet and unyielding. The air around them was cold and musty. From out of the fog, partially lit by moonlight, appeared a large silver counter with *The Red Frog Cafe* imprinted onto it. In front of the counter were three tall wooden bar stools.

A thin barman was standing behind the counter. He had grey skin, grey slicked-back hair, grey ears, grey eyes, and even a grey nose. Through his face and body, you could see the background behind him. Rita figured him for a ghost, but he seemed amiable. His smile was as thin as he was and his eyes twinkled.

'It's quiet tonight, Fritz?' Lester said, looking around.

The barman picked up a small glass and began to polish it. His smile turned into a friendly grin as he replied.

'It's been dead all night. Should pick up in a little while. Chance Fosbery is singing here tonight. Your timing is impeccable as always, Lester.'

'Chance Fosbery, eh? Sounds good. While we wait,

can you please make a milkshake for my friend? And give me a shot of the hard stuff on the rocks.'

'Sure thing,' Fritz replied, and he picked up a large milkshake glass. He walked towards Rita and looked over the bar at her. He rubbed the stubble on his face and removed a matchstick from the corner of his mouth. 'What flavour you want, slim?' he asked, his accent a slow southern American drawl.

'I'll have a chocolate milkshake, please.'

Fritz nodded and began to make the drinks.

Rita placed her backpack on the ground and climbed onto a stool next to Lester. 'Where exactly am I?'

'You're in a place known as Neon City. When you followed me through the arch in Morecambe, you invited yourself here.'

'And this is a city in England?'

Lester moved his head from side to side.

'America?'

'Nope, not there either. We're far away from both.'

'I can get back to Morecambe though?' Rita asked, now beginning to panic.

'Don't worry about that. You can go back anytime. And it will be the same time as when you left.'

'What do you mean by that?'

'When you come here, time in your world will stand still for you. If it was eight o'clock in Morecambe, it will still be that time when you return.'

'And on the same day?' Rita asked, both corners of her mouth turning up in a smile.

'The very same.'

'How is that possible?'

'It's magic,' Lester said, taking a sip of his double espresso coffee. 'Actually, it's more science than magic. Try to think of this place as being a twin of the Earth, but the people and places are somewhat different.'

'I still don't get it. Is there an app for it?' Rita asked, and she gripped the ice-cold milkshake glass and drank down the thick luscious mixture.

'Not that I'm aware of, but I can probably get you a book about it. How's the drink?'

'Delicious. Can I ask why you went to that castle? Was it to get some money?'

'Pretty much. I'm receiving some benefits while I look for another job.'

'But they're going to stop them now?'

'You don't miss a thing,' Lester said. He smiled and

finished the last of his bitter coffee. 'Yes, I've got two weeks to find a job or I'm done for.'

From behind them came an explosion of applause. Lester and Rita turned around. A large crowd was standing away from the bar. Their applause was focused on a large grey ghost who was waving at them. With his other hand, he wiped his forehead with a red handkerchief. A large spotlight lit him up.

Chance Fosbery was five foot nine and built like three safes stacked on top of one another. His grey afro hair, lit up by the spotlight, towered above his head and was threaded into a sharp square. He pushed his handkerchief into his suit pocket and picked up a microphone. As he opened his mouth, Rita noticed he had an emerald in one of his front teeth.

'Thank you, thank you all,' Chance said, bowing to the audience. 'It's good to see all you deadbeats again. I hope you've had a stiff drink and are ready for something to lift your spirits.' Chance's face smoothed out, and his deep booming voice began to sing:

41

*Ain't nobody tells me what to do,*
*Me and them folks are through,*
*I'm tired and drowned in advice,*
*And I ain't gonna say it twice,*
*Don't you tell me what to do.*

'What about starting your own business, Lester?'
Rita asked.

'Good idea, but I've no cash. I don't know what
business I could run if I did have the money.'

*Money talks to me at night,*
*Then my bills start to bite,*
*Trying hard to make a dollar last,*
*Never thinking of the past,*
*Folks tell me to make money,*
*But then I say don't be funny,*
*And please don't tell me what to do.*

'What were you doing before?'

'I put some money into a property business run by
a friend. It turned out to be a fake front for a criminal
scam. When the police arrested him, they took his
money and mine.'

'Where is he now?'

'He's somewhere. We lost touch and he set me back years. I don't want to talk to him again unless it's necessary.'

*I had an ugly pal in Delhi,*
*Some friends tried to tell me,*
*He was up to no good,*
*His empathy was like wood,*
*But I gave him the doubt,*
*Until I found out,*
*He was a jealous little fool,*
*Don't you tell me what to do,*
*Oh no, don't you ever tell me what to do!*

'That's a shame,' Rita said. 'Is that what you were thinking about when I saw you in Morecambe?'

'No. I just wanted to get out of this city for a day. But I have been wondering why some bad things happened in the past.'

'So you could learn from them?'

'You may have a point,' Lester agreed.

'Maybe now you just need a little help?'

'Possibly. Do you have something in mind?' he asked, clearing their glasses from the bar.

Rita looked over the bar at a skeleton that was dancing with a witch. The skeleton was agile and his feet moved in gentle circles, his bones clicking like a patient metronome. By comparison, the witch was heavy and clumsy. Every so often she lost her footing and the skeleton helped keep her upright. Eventually, he led her to a grave and a blanket of red mist appeared. When it had cleared, they were both gone. It was a macabre moment, and Rita wondered if either of them were ever really there.

# CHAPTER SEVEN

## Trouble in Mind

At eight o'clock in the morning, the shambling black-clad figure of Doctor Krauss opened an umbrella as a torrent of rain fell upon him. The clouds had appeared dark and ready to burst for some time.

Water was dripping through a small hole in Doctor Krauss's umbrella. It leaked onto his hand and ran down the inside of his white shirt arm. Under his other arm, he was carrying a black ledger containing a detailed report. He stopped at one point to pull his long black coat together, and to straighten a black cape that hung down to his waist.

As Doctor Krauss made his way along Tenth Street,

he could see the outline of Neon City's probation office. On reaching it, he pushed his way through the creaking red-pine entrance door. He folded his wet umbrella away and ran his fingers through his stringy white hair. He found the interview room and knocked on the door twice. A sharp robust voice told him to come in.

The voice belonged to a witch called Esmeralda Darkstone. She said: 'Doctor Krauss, thank you for taking the time to join us. I see you've brought the report you promised.'

'I certainly have,' Doctor Krauss said, dropping the heavy document onto a table which shook with the weight.

'Maybe you can save some time by giving us a summary of what you know?' Esmeralda asked, flicking a small piece of dust from her grey suit.

'I'm not much of a speaker,' Doctor Krauss said in a whiny voice with a hint of a German accent. 'I—'

'Please do your best,' she said, her one blue eye focusing on Doctor Krauss. The other eye was made of crystal and had been lost to a faulty potion.

'I suppose I should start at the beginning. I was appointed, some months ago, to be an acting

Custodial photograph

1. Surname

*Snyde*

2. Other names

*Ermington*

3. Description
Ghoulish demeanour
Piercing eyes
*Partial to a top hat*
→ Tall

Height
including
hat
approx
1.91m

2269617

psychiatrist to a prisoner known as Mr Ermington Snyde.'

'Doctor Krauss,' Esmeralda replied. 'What we need here today is simply a list of Mr Snyde's issues. Then your belief as to whether he should be free to re-join society.'

'Mr Snyde was presented to me due to his anti-social nature. He had spent a great deal of time in solitary confinement. When released into the main prison population he stopped talking to the other prisoners and the guards.'

'You were obviously concerned about that.'

'Of course. In our first meeting, he seemed to open up and told me he needed a stronger mind. I agreed to help him. But stressed he would have to answer as many of my questions as he could.'

'What questions were those?'

'Mr Snyde has a history of compulsive lying and delusions. His delusions are centred around his desire to give society meaning.'

'I see. In terms of his lies, did you get to the bottom of that?'

'Yes. He received a lot of abuse from his father. The—'

'Who was the father?'

'I can't confirm, as Mr Snyde refuses to name family members. We know that he was born in the year 1764 close to Moscow. With his accent and manners, I suspect he originates from aristocracy.'

'What does your intuition tell you about the abuse?'

'Possibly jealousy. Mr Snyde is exceptionally handsome; it could have provoked resentment in an ageing father. Due to that, I think Mr Snyde spent most of his time trying to get affection and respect. He admits his lies were designed to impress strangers. I believe he fits that model of behaviour. The simplest way to explain this is to say it is a personality disorder. Formed in childhood, it cannot be cured but can be managed. With therapy, such as mentalism, we can ask the patient to empathise with others. This is done by asking him to consider what others around him are thinking.'

Sitting next to Esmeralda was Mr Philip Aster, a wizard and a director of the Green Crane Museum. He ran a hand over his thick black dreadlocks. 'Mr Snyde has quite a history. Can you fill in the blanks?' he asked, in a sweet and flowery voice.

'Only a few,' Doctor Krauss said, opening his report to find a list of dates and places. He looked at them through his rounded spectacles which were perched on the end of his nose. 'While in Korea in 1910, Mr Snyde unwittingly became a prisoner of Japanese forces in the country. Although fluent in the Korean language, he gave his captors no details of how he came to be in the country. They tried to break him to get more information but couldn't put a dent in him. They resorted to isolating him in solitary confinement. That had, also, no effect. After six months they released him back into the main prison. He then worked in the prison library where, he says, he read a lot about Alexander the Great. He also studied the history of Japan and threw himself into learning the language. He began to converse with the prison guards fluently in their native language. It was then that the Japanese intelligence service took an interest in him. They released him to be trained. After that, he joined the Black Dragon Society. He became an expert at blending in and passing unnoticed. Also, he made himself a big player in the world of financial crime. From there he acquired the advanced skills of an assassin.'

'He gets around,' Esmeralda said, placing a hand on her green chin. 'Tell me, Doctor Krauss, do you think Mr Snyde has changed his ways at all?'

'He's made good progress and admitted his shortcomings. With therapy, we seem to have convinced him to stop lying. I have a few worries, particularly how he sees everything in terms of black or white. It's also dismaying that he seems to have cut many people out of his life over the years. However, I think being back in civilisation will complete his therapy. He'll have more of a chance to practise being social. I genuinely think he wants to contribute to society.'

'Is he able to contribute?' Mr Aster asked. 'His mind, is it broken or…'

'I can assure you his mind is razor-sharp. He can sit for hours and focus on one thing. He's not easily distracted. He has also acquired many skills over the years. The only question I want answering is how he's been alive for so—'

'But do you consider him to be potentially violent?'

'Oh no. I can assure you that Mr Snyde has been rehabilitated. He wouldn't hurt a fly or say boo to a zombie. From now on, he will show others nothing but love. He will treat everyone with respect and—'

'Thank you, Doctor Krauss,' Esmeralda said, looking at her watch. 'I have a botox appointment later this morning, so let's iron this out. Mr Aster, this fellow has been a danger to society and a reputed criminal. I'm willing to give him the benefit of the doubt. But what do *you* think should be done with Mr Snyde?'

'I say we subject him to a year on probation,' Mr Aster replied, stroking his greying beard. 'But if he commits another crime, annoys anyone or even utters an obscenity… he goes back to prison.'

'He has improved,' Doctor Krauss promised. 'He certainly changed his behaviour while in our solitary confinement section. So much so that he was given level three privileges, which included outgoing phone calls.'

'Promising. It sounds like we are all in agreement,' Esmeralda said, leaning closer to an old tape recorder. 'We therefore release Mr Ermington Snyde on today's date of January the thirteenth.'

# CHAPTER EIGHT

## The Asphalt Jungle

Lester and Rita were walking slowly along Scarlet Road in Neon City. It had been a wet morning and the black pavement was slick with rain. The area was teeming, with a dense population pushing its way through small spaces.

All around the sound of heavy industry thundered in the background. There was the clang of steel girders colliding and kinetic energy turned into ringing sound waves. They ripped through a carefully organised construction site that had been fenced off. Inside the steel circle, an old apartment building was being torn to the ground.

A witch in a smart business suit walked past Rita, who nodded as the green-faced lady smiled at her.

'My mum works in recruitment,' Rita said. 'She's always telling me people make mistakes when looking for a job.'

'Really, like what?' Lester replied, looking down at Rita's face which was serious with intent.

'Well, you need a good résumé first. Plus, she says applications are a waste of time and it's better to just knock on doors.'

'I'm not sure the police would like you doing that.'

'No, not like breaking in. Just visiting a company's office and introducing yourself.'

'That is a good idea, but I get nervous about such things.'

'But how will you ever get an interview if you don't introduce yourself?'

'I did have an interview a month ago for a job in a bank.'

'How did it go?' Rita asked, stepping out of the path of an oncoming white unicorn.

'Not good. I'm not sure I'm cut out for banking.'

'How come?'

'I'm too nice. Nice guys don't work in finance. They bleed honesty into its gutters.'

'Don't be so hard on yourself! I think you just need to do things differently.'

'You have to understand that being unemployed is a full-time job,' Lester said. 'What with applications and all that.'

'But you can't just quit.'

'I haven't quit. I've just learned to lower my expectations of life.'

'But everyone else has a job, Lester.'

'I'm not everyone. Besides, this culture is new to you at the moment.'

'What difference does that make?'

'It means you should tread softly and take it slow, to begin with. The honeymoon period doesn't last long in Neon City.'

'Fair enough, but you have to keep busy,' Rita said, feeling frustrated.

'It's busy this morning,' Lester replied, narrowly avoiding walking into a tall Tengu. It removed its Fedora hat and bowed to Rita. Its hair was slicked back and smelt of cheap hair tonic. As it leaned forward, she got a look at its foot-long red nose, and thick high white eyebrows. It rubbed its grey white moustache.

'Good morning. For two hundred yen, I can give you the winning—'

'Leave it, Frank,' Lester said to the Tengu. 'She's too young to play the lottery.'

The Tengu looked disappointed and carried on walking. His wooden geta sandals clip clopped away.

'I could have given the numbers to my mum!' Rita said.

'It wouldn't do any good. Frank hasn't picked any lucky numbers for a hundred years. He has a large divorce bill to pay off. If he could pick a winning ticket, he'd use it himself.'

'Too bad for him. For you, maybe we can make a résumé today and call into some offices?'

Lester did not respond; he was busy looking at a street vendor who was serving up sticky fried chocolate doughnuts.

'What do you think?' Rita asked, beginning to notice Lester was easily distracted.

'I think those doughnuts smell wonderful.'

'No, about getting a job.'

'To tell you the truth, Rita, I like to do things my

way. I know I'm a needle stuck in a groove, but the music will change for me soon enough.'

'Maybe you need some improvisation? Are you listening to me, Lester?'

Lester was looking away from Rita towards a crowd gathered in front of a shop across the road.

# CHAPTER NINE

## This Dragon for Hire

On the other side of Scarlet Road was a small dusty green shop. It was placed in-between two prominent, and much nicer shops called *The Old Thrift Shop* and *Dellarowe's*. Rita had to squint slightly to read the name of the green shop squeezed in the middle of the two. Its sign spelt out *Que's Palace*.

The tiny shop dealt exclusively with antiques and jewellery. At first glance, it appeared worn out and defeated like a rusty abandoned car. It also seemed to be damaged, with a broken steel front door lying on the ground.

Just in front of Que's Palace, a large crowd of onlookers were listening to a raging argument between a goblin and a member of the police force.

'What's going on over there?' Rita asked.

'Looks like a burglary to me,' Lester said. 'Come on, let's take a closer look.'

Mr Que, the large bald goblin who owned the damaged shop, continued to complain loudly. He was venting his frustration at a police inspector known as Donnelly.

Inspector Donnelly was a cyclops, with one eye in the middle of his forehead. His face was dark brown, with high cheekbones and a firm jaw. He wore a policeman's uniform of a blue shirt, blazer, tie, and black trousers. His physique was both flabby and muscular. It was the product of late-night stakeouts, coffee, and too much fast food.

As the goblin became increasingly animated, Donnelly responded by nodding his head every so often. His face had a sincere look of sympathy.

'And another thing!' Mr Que shouted, his voice beginning to squawk like a parrot's. 'Don't tell me there's nothing you can do! Finding antique swords can't be that difficult!'

61

'Calm down,' the inspector urged. 'We will do everything in our power to catch whoever did this.'

'What's going on?' Lester asked.

'One of your kind… a dragon, decided to steal sixteen expensive antique swords last night,' Donnelly said, in a condescending tone.

'How do you know a dragon like Lester did it?' Rita asked.

'The locks on the front door have been melted. It seems fair enough to assume a large and powerful dragon could manage that,' the inspector replied, in a hard clipped British accent.

'Let's test that theory of yours,' Lester said, and from out of his pocket he pulled a large magnifying glass. He then started to examine the broken steel door.

'This wasn't the work of a dragon.'

'Pshaw! What rubbish, where is your proof?' Donnelly said, leaning his body forward.

'Yes, how do you know?' Rita asked, surprised at his knowledge on such matters.

'Simple,' Lester said, putting his magnifying glass into Rita's hands. 'This door is made of steel. Extreme heat such as fire will create a build-up of carbon on the surface. This causes the metal to change colour to blue as the carbon leaves the surface. The door has turned no such colour, and it also appears pitted. Notice here,' Lester said, pointing at the damage.

'You're smarter than you dress,' Donnelly said. 'Maybe you can save my career by talking to the owner. Impress me by getting more information out of him than I could.' Donnelly pointed out the shop owner's name written in his notepad. 'While you're doing that, I'll get the forensics team to check the door.' With that said, he walked away to speak with his colleagues.

'You should work for the police,' Rita said and she looked at Lester.

'Maybe. Let's talk to the shop owner and see what he knows.'

'Mr Frederick Que, I believe?'

'Who wants to know and who wishes to be insulted?' the goblin replied, who was wearing jeans and a slack white T-shirt with *Don't Bother Asking for Credit* printed across it.

'Can I ask about the items which were stolen?'

'You can ask, but I would prefer it if you could arrange their return!' the goblin replied, small spider web wrinkles appearing around his nose.

'Perhaps I can,' Lester said. 'There were sixteen swords stolen in all. Were they the most high-priced swords in the shop?'

'Interesting, curiously interesting,' Mr Que replied. 'Wait here and I shall dig out my stock book.'

'With pleasure.'

'Why did you ask if they were the most expensive swords?' Rita asked, noticing that Donnelly's forensic officers were now checking the broken shop door.

'If someone decided to steal swords to use in a fight or a battle, they would choose the sturdiest and sharpest ones.'

'And?'

'And if the thief needed cash, he might decide to steal the most pricey swords so he could sell them.'

'You're good at this,' Rita said, genuinely impressed.

The goblin had returned with a heavy yellow file, tucked under his right arm, which he passed to Lester.

'You're right,' he said. 'Those swords were the

most expensive. They were nice items too. Black samurai swords with rubies and tiger eye gemstones in the handles.'

Lester's eyes flicked over the columns of numbers in the ledger.

'Interesting, Mr Que. How many of these swords could a human carry on their own?'

'I should say four at the most.'

'How do you think they would carry them?' Rita asked.

'They could carry two swords on each shoulder.'

Inspector Donnelly walked over to Lester, eyeing him sternly.

'Now, I will agree you are right about the melted door. But how were all sixteen swords carried away? No one person could carry all that on their own,' he said, brusquely.

'I spoke with Mr Que, and he said one person could carry four swords. Sixteen divided by four means we are looking for four humans.'

'That's clever,' Rita said.

'Yes, too clever,' Donnelly added, looking jealously impressed. 'But how do you know the criminals were human?'

'Because dragon fingerprints are triangular. Humans leave circular swirls on everything they touch. Didn't your forensics people see the human fingerprints on the door?'

'Sometimes my people are… it doesn't matter,' Donnelly replied, he pulled a pen from his pocket. He wrote his phone number out and added his signature to a small piece of paper. 'Here, this is my name and phone number. My badge number is three hundred and forty-one. Call me if you think up anything else, Mr Lester.'

'Will do,' the dragon said, with a hint of proud satisfaction in his voice. He tucked the paper into his wallet.

Mr Que ran a hand over his shiny bald green head. On his face was a look of surprise. 'You seem to be quite well informed, Mr Dragon. Were you in the police force yourself?' he asked.

'No. I'm well-read if that's any consolation to you.'

'Perhaps I could make you an offer for your skills,' Mr Que said, lowering his head and indicating Lester to follow him so they were out of Donnelly's earshot.

'What kind of offer?'

'I could give you an advance of eight thousand yen

now and another twenty thousand when you find my stolen swords.'

'Eight thousand, eh? In the detective profession, that's known as a retainer.'

'Yes, whatever. Are you interested or not?'

'Not a chance,' Rita said.

'What?' Lester gasped.

'Why not? What's the problem?'

'He's in great demand and does not come cheap. I think a retainer of one hundred thousand yen should be the price for a skilled private detective.'

'One hundred thousand yen!' Mr Que said as if he had been stabbed in the heart. 'I can't afford that. How about fifty thousand yen?'

'Don't be cheap,' Rita replied. 'A retainer of seventy-five thousand yen at least.'

'Seventy thousand yen and not one more or our deal is not going to happen.'

'I suppose you are a new client, so we can include a discount. However, we have to charge a ten per cent bonus on any items recovered.'

'Alright,' Mr Que agreed and reached into his pocket to retrieve his wallet. 'I suppose ten per cent of nothing will have to do. Here you go, seven hundred centuries,' he said, passing a large bundle of banknotes to Lester.

'See,' Rita said. 'That wasn't so difficult was it?'

'Just torture me next time,' Mr Que snapped, turning to walk back to his shop.

'Did you see all the cobwebs in his wallet?' Rita said, feeling a little taller.

'Seventy thousand yen,' Lester said, as he pocketed the money. 'I can hardly believe my luck. Why I... what's the matter with your face, Rita?'

'How much is seventy thousand yen worth?'

'A lot. Why do you ask?'

Rita looked Lester up and down. 'I was thinking we should get you some new clothes. And a new hat too.'

# CHAPTER TEN

## No Man so Fierce

An oven heat blew onto the maze-like streets of Neon City. The early morning rain, akin to a monsoon, had boiled into a sticky vapour.

The city's tropical weather system was cruel to visitors, and not forgiving to its citizens. It certainly took some getting used to, as did the labyrinth of streets. One wrong step could cost tourists hours of their day.

The man walking around Dangerous Corner made no stumbles. His thin lips parted occasionally, and he sucked fresh air through his sharp milk teeth. The wrinkles around his eyes were deep trenches and reminders of bad memories. He carried an aura of something wicked about him.

As the man reached the red paving stones of Himes Road, he glanced at his wristwatch. He narrowly avoided walking into a large troll that was wearing a gold shell-suit. The troll was on his morning jog and appeared upset by the interruption.

'Hey, watch where you're going!' the troll said.

The man said nothing. He came to a stop and looked across at the troll. His face was a blank neutral expression. For two minutes he stood in silence.

'Well, I suppose accidents happen,' the troll said. 'You have a nice morning,' he added and then jogged away.

The man, now crossing the road, spotted a large warehouse of earthy brick. He neatly stepped through its wooden entrance and stood under the cool shield of its roofing tiles. He straightened his black tie and ran a hand through his badly cut white hair.

Inside the warehouse, the view was one of busy efficiency. A small yellow forklift truck beeped impatiently as it reversed. It carried a pallet comprised of sandbags. In a small loading bay, two dwarves in blue uniforms unloaded the bags, lifting them carefully onto the back of a large delivery truck.

Shards of natural light from the loading bay lit up a dancing layer of dust in the air. From out of the light, a dwarf wearing an orange hard hat and carrying a clipboard approached.

'Help you with something?' he asked.

'I want to place an order and I need the goods quickly,' the man said, his voice sounding like rocks being torn apart.

'We can surely help you with that,' the dwarf said, his thick stumpy fingers pointing left. 'Walk through that exit, and then out into the lumber yard. There's a small office there. Doris will help you place an order.'

The man nodded slightly and left the dwarf without saying thank you. As he walked through the middle of cut Jeffrey-pine timber, he smelt the scent of vanilla. Ten feet away from the wood, he saw a small plastic shack.

Inside her office, Doris the mermaid smiled at the stranger. She had been typing invoices at her desk, sitting in a half barrel of water.

'Good morning, Sir,' she said. 'How can I help?'

The man did not say good morning back, and

Doris's thick red scaly tail dropped beneath the surface of the water.

'How soon can you get this?' the man asked, his lips stretching across his small teeth. His twisted lumpy fingers dropping something onto the plywood desk.

Doris unfolded a piece of paper and read the contents of a handwritten list.

'I can get that much concrete anytime. Do you have enough room to store it?' she asked, her large orange eyes focused elsewhere.

'More than enough,' the man said, throwing a large wad of banknotes on Doris's desk.

'Your name for the order please?'

'Marvin. Make it out to Mr Marvin.'

Doris nodded and asked no more questions.

# CHAPTER ELEVEN

## Hello, My Lovely

Rita Wong looked into the afternoon sky. The sun shone brightly. The clouds had evaporated and a cool breeze blew. In front of her stood a large mansion, which had been built at enormous expense. She could see the bricks were composed of platinum and the window panes were made of gold.

At the entrance, two large wrought iron gates were open. Both of them displayed the motif of a serpent. Behind the gates was a yellow brick driveway.

However, the most impressive sight was the front door. It was a large block of silver embedded with red and green jewels. From a distance, the mansion looked like a piece of jewellery a giant might wear. The property was located on Riverside Drive in Neon City and was called *Priceless House*.

'Do you think he's at home?' Rita asked.

'Baron Stanley Chang?' Lester replied. 'I hope so. He's supposed to be the top man in the antique business. Judging by this place he's done well for himself. Do you think I'll make a good impression on him?' he asked.

Rita glanced at Lester's clothes. He was now wearing a charcoal trench coat, a white shirt with an emerald-green tie, black trousers, and black lace up shoes. On his head was a black British bowler hat, which she thought was quite stylish and had insisted he buy.

'You look like a million dollars, you'll cut the mustard.'

'I think I'll need more than a million to do that here. If I'm lucky I might get a cup of coffee. Come on, let's say hello.'

Lester and Rita walked to the front of the mansion and banged the knocker against the silver door twice. The door swung open by itself and they were both left staring at an empty hallway.

'Shall we go in?' Rita asked, nervously.

'I suppose so,' Lester replied, sounding twice as nervous.

They entered the hallway, and both of them jumped when the large front door slammed shut behind them.

Rita took a quick look around. Two beige couches were lining both inner walls. In the middle of the hallway, a large staircase led up to another floor. Hanging over it was a chandelier designed in concentric circles that glowed with amber light. When she looked behind her, she saw that a walnut-wood bookcase had been built around the front door. It was stacked with classic novels and maps.

From above, Rita could hear a melodic tune being played on a saxophone. It suddenly stopped and a woman dressed in a white crepe cocktail dress appeared. She approached them, drifting down the stairs like a sweet and eloquent wind. Lester and Rita couldn't help staring at her. She was incredibly beautiful with large brown eyes, pencil-thin curved eyebrows, skin as smooth as glass, and thick autumn-toned hair held back by a jewelled headband.

The woman walked down the stairs elegantly and made the act of walking into an art form. Her perfume, a heady smell of lavender and juniper, was hypnotic.

'How may I help you?' she asked in a husky voice.

'We would like to speak with Baron Stanley Chang, please,' Lester said.

'Everyone would like to speak with my father,' she replied. 'May I ask the nature of your business?'

'There was a burglary at an antique shop in the city. I'd like the Baron's opinion on the items taken. And if he would know someone interested in the stolen goods.'

'Just to be clear, you are looking for someone who would buy stolen antiques?'

'Yes.'

'And your name, Mr?'

'Thyme, my name is Lester Thyme.'

'I see. That's a nice outfit you're wearing, Mr Thyme,' the woman said, removing her headband and shaking her hair loose.

'Thank you,' Lester said, smiling from ear to ear.

'Have you had that trench coat for some time?'

'Yes. A long time.'

'Then you might want to remove the price tag from it.'

'Ah, I sometimes miss the obvious,' Lester said, finding the offending tag and pulling it off the coat.

The woman's eyes narrowed. She removed a lipstick from her pocket and applied it lightly to her mouth.

'Very well. I'm confident my father would be more than willing to speak with you. Please allow me to introduce myself first. My name is Delilah Chang, and I manage our shops in New York and Paris. May I ask your profession?' she asked, widening her gaze at Lester.

'I have quite a range. I'm a jack of all trades and master of none. To be honest for some time I've been unem—'

'He's a private detective,' Rita interrupted.

Lester turned and nodded ever so slightly.

'Interesting,' Delilah replied, but she did not make eye contact with Rita. Her eyes were aimed at Lester.

Rita turned to look at Lester's face. He was staring at Delilah as if in a trance.

'We are here on official business,' Rita said, worrying that their bluff had been seen through.

'Truly fascinating,' Delilah replied, brushing a stray hair from her forehead. 'But I don't believe I know your office. Could you enlighten me with its name, Mr Thyme?'

Rita saw a nervous look pass over Lester's face and he seemed lost for words.

'It's called Wong and Thyme: Private Detective Agency,' Rita said. 'We're new to the city.'

'Would you be Miss Wong in that case?'

'Yes, indeed I am.'

'You seem rather young to be a partner in a business as rough as yours can sometimes be?'

'She's my accountant,' Lester said, appearing to have come out of a daydream.

'I suppose that adds up,' Delilah replied, nodding her head. 'Now, if you will excuse me, I will send my father down to you. Delightful to meet you, Lester and Rita.' With that, Delilah turned and walked back up the stairs just as gracefully as she had descended them. Lester watched on and was captivated until her slender frame vanished from sight.

'Very very nice to meet you,' he whispered.

Rita heard his compliment and smiled to herself.

'You're in love with her, aren't you?' she asked,

then pushed her spectacles up while looking at him.

'Er, no. She's just a potential suspect,' he said. 'I think she's up to something and I'm going to keep an eye on her.'

'You seemed to have two eyes on her a minute ago.'

'Stop suggesting things.'

At that moment, a portly round man dressed in an excessive designer suit began to walk down the staircase. He had spiky black hair, thick chubby cheeks, and an unusually small nose.

Lester and Rita noticed he was not as classy or as elegant as his daughter. He descended the stairs like a jellyfish pulled out of the sea.

Lester was about to speak, but the Baron waved his arms wildly in the air to stop him. He then threw a question in his direction.

'Your business here today?'

'We're private detectives, investigating stolen antique swords.'

'In that case, I will give you two minutes of my time, and if you should take up one-second longer of it, I will be forced to charge you for the

79

inconvenience. Time is money to a gentleman like myself. Particularly as I'm drowning in paperwork today.' He pulled out a gold stopwatch to time their conversation.

Rita found it hard to believe the Baron was a gentleman, his behaviour seemed more like that of a gangster. She noticed Lester had decided not to waste one second of the two minutes.

'Sixteen antique swords were stolen from a shop in the city. All steep in price. Are they in demand in the antique market presently?' Lester asked.

'Things are currently uncertain,' the Baron said, putting his hands together in a steeple. 'And people like quality over quantity. If trouble is likely, better always to trust good craftsmanship.'

'The swords stolen were the most costly in the shop. Would you agree that only an expert in antiques could make such a distinction?'

'I think I understand,' the Baron said. 'Are you saying an expert was in on the burglary?'

'That's exactly what I'm saying.'

'Whoever would do such a thing?'

Lester went quiet for a moment.

'Good gracious!' the Baron said, his eyes lighting

81

up with fury. 'Are you accusing me of thievery? You're out of order, Mr Trout!'

'Actually, my name is Thyme. And I'm not accusing you of anything. I'm merely asking if you know another antique dealer who has quick hands.'

'I understand now,' the Baron said, letting out a loud breath. 'The only person I can think of who might be a common thief is one of my competitors, Atkins, a Mr Walter Atkins. For years his business has been struggling, and I have the feeling he is envious of my success. Perhaps you should visit him and subject him to questioning.'

The Baron appeared less nervous and he began to glare at Rita.

'Is she your silent partner? Cat got your tongue, girl?' he said and then laughed.

'No, I was just listening closely to your story, Mr Baron. I wonder, does Mr Atkins make a habit of dealing in swords?'

'No, he sells antique furniture.'

'Don't you think it's strange that Mr Atkins would steal swords, items he doesn't usually sell?'

'And as he only has experience in furniture,' Lester

added, 'how could he know which swords were worth a lot of money?'

'Yes, but who knows what goes on in that dwarf's mind?' the Baron said, looking at his stopwatch. 'Your two minutes are up, you must go. Have a good day!' And he turned and ran up the stairs.

'He moves quickly for a man his size,' Lester said. 'I don't think his daughter got his looks.'

'Or his charm,' Rita replied.

# CHAPTER TWELVE

## Repeat Performance

'What do we do now?' Rita asked. Lester had said nothing but there appeared to be something on his mind.

'I was thinking about your question to the Baron.'

'What about it?'

'I don't think Mr Atkins would steal anything. I've known him for years; all the furniture in my house was bought from his shop. For that reason, I want to hear his opinion. I think the Baron is hiding something. His answers were slightly offbeat.'

'I agree with you there.'

Walking away from Priceless House, they took a

left onto River Boulevard and headed for South Street where Mr Atkins's shop was located. South Street was lined with simple grey brick shops fitted with roller shutters that looked like shoe boxes with metal fronts. The street was quiet as if it had been forgotten. It appeared to be a perfect place for incognito ghosts to shop. There was a boring silence in the air, and the feeling of an era coming to an end. The only colour onsite was a group of pink lilies growing in a gutter above the shop front.

'Here it is. Number six hundred and fifteen,' Lester said, pointing to a shop labelled *Hammer-Time*. Its roller shutter had been pulled clean off, and there was a beaten and melted front door lying in the street.

Lester saw Inspector Donnelly listening to Mr Atkins's grievances.

'It never ceases to amaze,' Donnelly said. 'Every time a crime has been committed you turn up like a blue note, Mr Lester. Do you have psychic powers of some kind? If so, perhaps you can tell us who made Mr Atkins's stock and tools disappear.'

'Have they been set on fire?' Rita asked.

'No they haven't,' Mr Atkins grumbled, in a broad

Scottish accent. 'But if they had, that would at least give me a reason why they're no longer here.'

Mr Atkins was a short and stocky dwarf. His face was tough, hard, and imposing. The kind even a swarm of bees would avoid.

'Any evidence?' Lester asked Donnelly.

'Nothing. Not a vegan sausage. My forensics team has gone over the area spot by spot. They can't find anything either.'

For the next few minutes both Lester and Rita searched the same area for clues, and they also found nothing of any value.

'I don't believe this,' Rita said.

'Neither do I,' Donnelly replied. 'The crime scene is identical to the burglary at Mr Que's shop: one damaged front door, the locks of which have been melted. I've no doubts that both burglaries were perpetrated by the same villains.'

'Mr Atkins, do you have any known enemies at the moment?' Lester asked.

'None that I can think of. Although I'm often rude to double glazing salesmen,' he added, the lines around his eyes contracting like razor wire.

'Have you heard of Baron Stanley Chang?'

'Oh, you mean "Brilliant" Chang? Yes, I know that scoundrel,' Mr Atkins replied, his amber eyes moving to focus on Lester.

'Careful what you say,' Donnelly said. 'The Baron is a man of good character. I don't think you should say such things about him in public.'

'Alright, yes, I have heard of the Baron,' Mr Atkins replied, folding his arms across his chest.

'And the Baron certainly knows you,' Lester said. 'He suggested that you might be in the market for some stolen items: sixteen antique swords.'

'The flipping cheek of it! Did he say that?'

'He did indeed.'

'That smug bighead has been running a smear campaign against me for years!' Mr Atkins erupted, a vein in his neck swelling up like a hosepipe. 'He has told all kinds of lies about me to discredit my reputation. He is a jealous and greedy man.'

'Do you have any proof of your allegations?'

'I was thinking the same thing,' Donnelly added.

'No I don't,' Mr Atkins admitted. 'But if you were to ask in the right places, you'll find out exactly how he feels about me.' He pummelled his right fist into his left palm.

'Alright, tough guy, calm down,' Donnelly warned. 'Sounds like the bromance is over,' he joked.

After looking over the crime scene once again, Rita was dismayed there were no clues to the thieves' identities. She began to feel tired and covered her mouth to conceal a yawn.

'I think we had better get you back home for a rest,' Lester said.

'That probably is a good idea. We've had such a nice day out.'

'Haven't we just? Nothing like a couple of burglaries to brighten up a day.'

'Maybe. But what's all this about?' Rita asked. 'Tools, furniture, and swords?'

'I don't know. But it will make sense soon enough and keep for tomorrow. Come on, let's get you home.'

'I think Mr Atkins faked the burglary at his shop,' Rita said, putting her backpack over her shoulder.

'You think he stole from himself?'

'I do. I understand you've known him for a long time, but the people you least expect are often guilty.'

'Maybe you've been watching too many movies,' Lester said and straightened his hat.

When Rita got home, she explained to her mother

she was tired and for that reason hadn't gone to the library. Her mother suspected she had a cold, and agreed she should go to bed.

Rita lay on her stomach in bed and started to sketch a picture of her emerald ring. However, she was exhausted. Sleep soon overcame her, and she fell into a deep slumber.

# CHAPTER THIRTEEN

## Sorcerer

A warm light wind brushed against Rita Wong's ears carrying the sound of a bell. Her eyes then snapped open. She was standing and holding a vertical metal pole. Under her feet was a colourless vinyl floor. Glancing to her left she saw a large windowpane. Outside and engulfing the distance was a large futuristic city.

Looking around, Rita realised she was travelling on a train. As the journey was smooth, she let go of the cold pole and walked closer to the window. Beneath her, the floor quivered in a slow tempo.

The view of the city through the window was a drab one of black and white. The sky above it was clouded and filthy, almost blurred. Rita turned to look at the interior of the train. It was also shaded in inky blacks and fluid whites, with no colour. She wondered if her spectacles were dirty and reached into her pocket for a cloth. As she began wiping them, Rita noticed the lenses of the spectacles were now mirrors.

'Strange, are these mine?' she asked herself.

'No need to worry,' a voice behind her said.

Rita turned to see a tall broad man dressed in black. He had slicked his hair away from his handsome face. When he spoke again she noticed two sharp canine teeth protruding from his mouth.

'Your train always runs on time,' the man said, before disappearing into a puff of white smoke.

Before Rita could consider who had been speaking to her, a loud beeping noise travelled through the compartment. A polite voice followed, 'Would all passengers please ensure they collect their belongings before leaving the train. We wish you a pleasant day and hope your journey with us has been an enjoyable one.'

Rita checked to see if she had any luggage. All she had were her clothes and nothing more.

The train stopped and the compartment door hissed as it opened. Through the door was a set of metal steps that led down to a concrete platform. Rita made her way down the steps and into a bright sunny day. The humidity was pleasant but she soon realised she was alone on the platform. She saw no maps or information to guide her. Across the wind, she once again heard the sound of a bell.

'Where is that coming from?' Rita wondered.

Turning to the north, she saw a large concrete footbridge that appeared to be straddling a river. From the same direction, she began to hear a series of clicking sounds.

'The bridge it is then I suppose,' Rita thought, and she began walking northwards.

The river beneath the bridge contained water that was deep black like volcanic glass. Rita peered over the side of the bridge and noticed that the water was perfectly calm. She could see a reflection of herself wearing the mirrored spectacles on the surface. Once again, she heard the sound of a bell and the clicking noise.

Rita came to the end of the bridge. As she walked into a large cityscape, she could smell petrol. Passing through an abandoned market covered in soot, she was briefly shadowed by a canvas tarpaulin. Flowing around it were crowded streets lined with a tangle of high-rise buildings. The architecture used on each building was different, and it created a jumble of periodic styles. From a previous study of the subject, she recognised constructions from the 1940s through to the present day and beyond.

'But they're all in black and white,' Rita said aloud.

As well as no colour, the streets of the city contained no real plant life. Every so often a hawthorn tree had been planted. Yet their trunks were covered with oily plug sockets, and their branches dripped with black electric cables. Above them hung streetlights of chrome and plastic with neon electrified glass tubes glowing stark white. Inside the tubes was ionised carbon dioxide gas. A landscape dominated by the contrast of harsh light and electric corrosion.

Rita held a cable coming from a tree. It felt warm, and when she let go it left a thick grimy oil on her hand. She continued walking and noticed that the buildings were becoming closer to one another.

They almost fought for the sun like flowers in a garden. Each skyscraper was labelled with the logo of a corporation. The names read Ramsay, Travers, and Claude. At the end of the street, one hexagon-shaped building loomed above all the others. Rita was sure she could hear the clicking noise coming from somewhere inside it.

Before Rita could move, she felt her t-shirt start to become damp. Small splotches of black oil were staining her clothes. She placed a hand on her trouser leg and realised it was petrol. The sky above her had darkened with exhaust fumes and black snow. The effect, and smell, were overpowering. She decided to head inside the hexagon building for cover.

As Rita got closer she could see the entrance arch was dressed with black roses. A set of white stone steps led up to a set of black double doors. She once again heard the sound of a bell as she rang a buzzer. The double doors immediately opened for her. Stepping inside, Rita walked past a small bar area and into a study room. In the corner, there was a large wooden desk.

Behind it, reclining in a chair, was a man reading a newspaper.

Rita rubbed her chin nervously and said: 'Excuse me.'

The man dropped his newspaper. He looked at Rita and removed a small clay pipe from his mouth. He was just about forty years old, with straight receding black hair which he had combed to one side. He was wearing a smoking jacket, a white shirt, and a grey silk tie. A small oil lamp lit up his waxy face.

'The lady is waiting for you upstairs,' the man said, pointing to an elevator door to the left of his desk. He then placed his pipe back in his mouth, lifted his newspaper and acted as if she was no longer there.

Rita walked over to the elevator door. Within the chrome door was a set of vertical lines and an image of the sun in the centre. The door opened and Rita stepped in. As the elevator revved into life, she noticed that one side of it was made from plexiglass. It offered a more intense view of the industrial environment around the building. Rita saw flashes of blue lights between buildings, and she began to feel more isolated.

Turning away from the plexiglass, Rita caught a glimpse of herself in a mirror. She stepped closer to it and realised her clothes had changed. She now wore a black blazer and tie together with an ankle-length black skirt. Her face looked pale and she was desperate to flee the claustrophobic elevator. Above her, a speaker gave out a gentle ping, and the door opened.

Stepping out of the elevator, Rita entered an unlit office. Straight ahead of her was a woman seated behind a desk. Her fingers were pneumatically banging on the keys of a vintage Hermes typewriter.

'I shall be with you in one minute, Rita. Why don't you take a seat over here,' the woman announced, pointing a finger at a chair in front of her desk. She then looked down at the typewriter and once again her fingers hammered the keys. Every so often, a small bell on the typewriter rang out.

Rita stepped farther into the room and walked as slowly as she could. Above her was an arched ceiling. It was held in place with delicate aluminium ribs decorated with diamonds. Within the ceiling were two stained glass panels. One depicted a skeleton and another a black unicorn. Her eyes then flicked down and at the woman. She was continuing to type, and Rita noticed she was attired in a black silk business suit. The woman appeared to be in her early thirties.

'I take it Mr Sherlock Holmes told you where I was?' the woman asked, looking up from her typewriter.

'He is… I mean, yes he did,' Rita replied.

'Why don't you take a seat? Please,' the woman said and opened her left palm. Across it was a small tattoo of a heart.

Rita sat down and the woman leaned her slim figure across the desk. Her hair was a cloud of thick jet black held in place by a brown tiger eye clasp. The lips of her mouth parted and a voice sweet and dark like chocolate asked: 'Would you mind taking your spectacles off? So that I can see your face more clearly.'

'I can't see without them,' Rita replied.

'I understand, but please take them off. Even if only for a moment.'

Rita nodded her head. As she removed her spectacles everything in the room turned to colour. The desk in front of her was yellow-brown and made from poplar wood. She could see that the typewriter was olive green. The lowered blinds in the room were glowing with orange where the sun was trying to break through them. Most noticeable of all was the large silver chain the woman was wearing around her neck, at the end of which was a gold valve. It shimmered from a low ceiling light above it.

'This is a dream isn't it?' Rita asked.

'Perhaps a dream within a dream,' the woman replied.

'I can't see anything without my—'

'You don't need your spectacles to see what I want to show you,' the woman said, and she reached into a drawer in her desk. From out of it she pulled a thin brown card folder. Her nimble fingers opened it and removed a single sheet of paper. 'Now, let's see,' the woman announced. 'Rita Wong, British born and current resident of Morecambe. Your native language is English, which is the only language you currently speak. Although born in England, you moved to Hong Kong three years ago but have now returned. Some knowledge of architecture, and some artistic skill. Yes. You do like nice clean lines, don't you? Although, you have no martial arts skills to speak of, and no... it says here that you don't know how to program a computer. Is that right?'

'I don't,' Rita replied.

'Well, so much for stereotypes,' said the woman and she put the paper into its folder and back on her desk.

'I hate to be rude,' Rita said, 'but who exactly are you?'

'Oh, of course. I forget formalities,' the woman replied and placed her hands together in a steeple. 'My name is Lady Malia Bricolage. You could say I'm a woman of investments. I've brought you here as I'm considering financing you, Rita. What would you say if I could return you and your family to Hong Kong?'

'I'd say that's impossible.'

'Anything is possible. Especially with the friends I have. Why don't you take a look out of the window to your right?'

Rita stood up and away from her chair. She walked across a thick red carpet. At the window, she lifted the Venetian blinds and looked out. Down below, she could see the chaotic streets of Hong Kong. It seemed cleaner than the last time she had been and almost more beautiful. She was certain she could also smell dim sum and milk tea.

'What do you think?' Lady Bricolage's voice rang out behind her.

'I think I'm in a dream and about to wake up,' Rita replied.

'Not yet. Not just yet. Please come over here and take a look out of this window.'

Rita walked to the left of the room. She could see Lady Bricolage standing tall next to a walnut bookcase in the shape of an oil pump. It contained books by John Stuart Mill, Ayn Rand, and Richard Weaver.

Rita stood to the side of the bookshelf and looked out of the window. Lady Bricolage smiled and said: 'Maybe you could own Hong Kong, Rita. And also one of these.'

Out of the window, Rita could see the black obsidian of space. In the centre, the orange-red of planet Mars glowed. To the right of it was the yellow radiance of Saturn. On the left was the white, red, brown, yellow, and orange of Jupiter.

'That's quite an offer, Miss Bricolage,' Rita replied, her expression one of awe. 'But what exactly do you want in return?'

Kneeling slightly, Lady Bricolage patted Rita's left shoulder. 'All my friends call me Malia, as shall you. And all I want is for you to never return to Neon City or Lester Thyme.'

'Then the answer is no,' Rita replied and folded her arms across her chest. Her eyebrows raised together and her profile became one of stern defiance.

'Don't be too hasty,' Lady Bricolage said, placing her other hand on Rita's right shoulder, 'you are a social outcast, but also a realist underneath. You can't go through life in the shadow of that naive bungler.'

'He's not a bungler,' Rita replied. 'Besides, I'm just helping him. He's doing okay by himself right now.'

'No, he's not. He's just your silly inept sidekick, a ridiculous cliché with a tail. But you're different, Rita. Reality doesn't faze you, does it? You know what happens to people who try to help others. They fail. And no one believes they're being genuine anyway. Helpers miss out on the best in life.'

'Maybe I should be going now?'

'Yes, you can take the time to reconsider my offer.'

'I already said the answer is no,' Rita replied and put her spectacles back on.

'Think about it. If you don't, I'll have to visit Lester Thyme myself. That will have one of two results. Either I'll make him my fool, or I'll kill him.'

'What's Lester ever done to you? If you try to hurt him, I'll—'

'Goodbye, Rita,' said Lady Bricolage dissolving into a veil of crimson red smoke. Rita began to cough and was still coughing when she woke up at home.

# CHAPTER FOURTEEN

## While the City Sleeps

There is a patient silence in the early hours of the morning. While people sleep comfortably in their beds, the trees move gently from side to side in the wind. Birds peck at lawns hoping to catch dozy worms while wild hares sit and listen for the rest of the world to rise. Above them a cold mist circles and waits for the sun to warm the ground. When the air temperature is comfortable enough, the mist pleasantly evaporates.

Emerging from the mist was a nice cosy little house located on the corner of Rivington Street where it meets Clinton Avenue. Inside it, Ermington Snyde was enjoying the silence. He had woken, as usual, at five o'clock that morning. For half an hour, he had sat drinking Earl Grey tea and shaping his thoughts so that they had a purpose. From six o'clock he had practised an ancient martial art. Between seven and eight o'clock he had read poetry while eating porridge with blueberries. His morning activities were then concluded with a walk to sync his mind and body with nature.

While in prison, Ermington would normally write for several hours each day. He maintained that discipline and produced biographies on William Blake, Byron, and Emperor Hadrian. Due to the quality of his writing, he had been invited to speak at the University of Manchester. Although the invitation was later cancelled when it was discovered that Ermington had tried to steal one of Blake's paintings from the Manchester Art Gallery.

Since his release from prison, Ermington had decided to use his afternoons for appointments and social calls. Today was no exception. He had reserved time to call unannounced on an old friend in Neon City. It would be a surprise to his friend but he thought that best considering the aim of his visit.

Ermington placed a brown diamond ring on the third finger of his right hand. He then put on his black top hat and checked his appearance in the mirror. Before leaving, he circled the date of January the fourteenth on his wall calendar. Closing his back door, he walked out onto Newstead Street. As he strolled along, he took in the smells of coffee and freshly baked bread coming from hot ovens.

Giving in to temptation, Ermington called into a Japanese bakery. He emerged with a Melonpan and a cup of hot chocolate. As he bit into it, the sweet bun split as the cookie crust broke with a crunch. He washed it down with the frothy hot chocolate, its surface slick with caramel syrup.

'Beats cold porridge in prison,' Ermington said and began heading for the north of Neon City.

# CHAPTER FIFTEEN

## Fallen Angel

Kim Park could not sleep. She shifted around in her coffin once more, but it was no good. Her mind, a whirlwind of the past, would not shut down into sleep. It was then that she heard the banging. At first, she ignored it. She knew that she was not due to start work for another four hours. However, the banging continued and took on a melodic pattern. This made her even angrier. Eventually, she relented and threw open her coffin. She was ready to blame her sleeplessness on the offending caller.

'Who in this city do you think...' As Kim stopped

in mid-sentence, her bottom lip began to quiver and then her lips closed in silence.

Ermington Snyde looked at her, smiled, and smelled a red orchid he had tucked under the lapel of his grey pinstripe suit.

'Yesterday, I went to Agra,' he said. 'I saw the inside of the Taj Mahal. It is inlaid with gemstones that light up at night. They radiate beautiful colours, but none of them affected me as much as your eyes.'

'I think you'll have to do better than that,' Kim said, her almond eyes looking like they were on fire.

'My technique is a tad rusty,' Ermington said.

'At your age, it's not likely to improve. And besides, talk is cheap.'

'People who've spent time in solitary confinement might disagree with you.'

'I've spent a large portion of my life locked in a box, so I speak from experience,' Kim replied.

'Maybe you need to get out more.'

'What? And meet another man like you?'

'I suppose I did let you down.'

'You suppose right,' Kim said, folding her arms across her chest. 'Where have you been anyway?'

'Detained at someone's pleasure. But now free

to enjoy leisure,' Ermington replied, his voice a patchwork of tones from around the globe. Every word he spoke was in a different accent, such as Russian, French, and even Singlish. The effect on the listener was hypnotic and pleasing to the ear.

'Take off your hat,' Kim said. When he did so, she looked upon him and wondered what the secret of his eternal youth was. His thick tufts of wavy brown hair were bright and shiny, while his soft skin was youthfully fresh as always.

Kim Park had been ready to shout and scream at Ermington Snyde. She even considered clawing at that exquisite face of his. Instead, she managed to compose herself. She looked into his violet eyes. His pale face was slashed by streaks of light from nearby candles.

'What do we do now?' she asked.

'Let's go for a walk,' Ermington replied.

# CHAPTER SIXTEEN

## Sin Galore

Kim Park was watching the roulette wheel spin for the fifth time. Once again the circle twirled and the colours began to blend. A small white ball travelled anti-clockwise against the wheel head. It shot along in its track set within the bowl. The inevitability of speed and gravity eventually disturbed the ball's motion. Its journey was upset when it careened and then crashed into a deflector. It tumbled into the wheel head where it rolled up and down several times before narrowly avoiding a red pocket. By pure luck, it bounced out and settled into a black pocket marked with the number thirteen.

Both corners of Ermington Snyde's mouth turned upwards into a smile. He looked down as a large pile of red money chips was pushed towards him.

'Sir wins again,' a smartly dressed croupier said, her thin smile fading.

'Haven't you punished them enough for one night?' Kim Park asked, looking bored. She leaned forward, placed both hands on her knees and whispered in Ermington's ear: 'You know I don't like being stuck indoors at night.'

Ermington lifted his top hat slightly, nodded, and collected his money chips. He carried them over to a casino cashier who sat in an enclosed metal cage. As well as his roulette chips, Ermington handed over a large black one-hundred-thousand-dollar plaque. After cashing the chips in, he stuffed the Singaporean dollars into his pockets.

'I think you've forgotten how to enjoy winning,' he said to Kim Park.

She responded by looking at their surroundings. Ahead of her was a line of silver slot machines. They were humming melodically to entice their victims to spend every dollar they had. Sitting on stools in front of them were well-dressed but soulless humans. They pumped dollar after dollar into addictive games of poker and spinning pieces of fruit. The players stared at the game screens as if hypnotised by mirrors that could show the future. The machines looked like metal tombstones in an electric graveyard. Kim felt ill at ease at the noise and bright lights of the scene in front of her.

'No one in here is a winner,' she said to Ermington, surprised at his attraction to the gold room.

'Maybe not,' Ermington replied. 'But money is money. It's unpleasant to be without it.'

'Walking in the night is pleasant and free,' Kim said. 'It's where you find something priceless: peace of mind.'

'My mind has never been peaceful. And my night vision has never been good either.'

'Maybe you need to open your eyes wider.'

'Perhaps.'

They walked out of the reflective glass and harsh steel casino, its gaudy gold sign spelt out *Poker Palace*. The exterior street was spotless and covered with pink paving. Exotic grey palm trees swayed gently in the warm wind, and Ermington walked slowly at

Kim's side. He said nothing and looked as if he was elsewhere.

'You always think too much,' Kim Park said, swaying from side to side in her long black silk dress. She smiled and her eyes seemed to regain their mischievousness of former years.

'Too much time spent alone.'

'Really, Ermington. I thought you were tougher than that?'

'So did I. But life behind bars can be rough.'

'What kept you going?'

'Thinking of you,' he said. 'I've seen this moment in my dreams. Spending time with you and feeling refreshed afterwards. Your good looks are a warm liqueur for the soul.'

'Oh, I am a good looker,' Kim said, rubbing her small chin with her left hand. 'But I'm also expensive. Are you sure you can afford me?'

'I'd rob every bank in the world. Steal every gem and con every billionaire to get you back.'

'I'm not a lucky number, Ermington. Being with me is no simple game of chance. It takes a lot of work.'

'I'd break my back under the load.'

'I expect you to, my dear,' Kim said, her eyes

scanning a crowd of young people walking towards them. She noticed a couple holding hands and looking into each other's eyes. Their clothes were the same colour. They also wore matching square spectacles. It made Kim smile, and she took Ermington's hand in hers.

'I want a platinum diamond engagement ring on my finger,' she said.

'You'll get one. I promise,' Ermington said.

'I also need security. I'm tired of day jobs and taking orders.'

'I'm working on it. It'll take time, but I'll make you a lady of leisure.'

'Sounds promising,' Kim replied, looking to her left at a woman handing her child ice cream. 'However, I expect you to make me your whole world.'

'That's a tall order.'

'Then you better put your chef's hat on, and put it together.'

'I suppose I'll have to,' Ermington said.

Kim broke away from him before he could kiss her. She continued to hold his hand and they sat together on a small bench. In front of them was a view of the light blue waters of the marina.

'Why did you come back to me?' Kim asked.

Before Ermington could reply, a large machine shuddered to life. It began to emit blue oily bubbles which floated over their heads. Ten metres out in the marina, a wall of water rose from powerful spray jets. A flurry of white light was then projected onto the widescreen of liquid. It displayed a colourful short film of a couple singing together. Their voices sang softly and Kim leaned against Ermington.

Deep inside, Kim Park began to feel younger. She thought of all the hours she had wasted in a regimented and unprofitable office job. At her side, Ermington Snyde tried to answer her question. She placed a finger on his lips before he could speak. Then she gently kissed him on the cheek.

'Welcome back, handsome,' Kim Park said, and she then let go of all the years of hurt.

# CHAPTER SEVENTEEN

## Crime Wave

In Neon City the bright sun shone as Lester and Rita strolled along Brown Derby Road. It was in the east of the city, and close to the docks. The smell of seaweed rode the warm air.

Earlier that morning, Lester and Rita had endlessly debated their case over two hot chocolates. They were still no nearer to making sense of what their investigation was all about. They had then decided they should take the rest of the day off to relax their minds. Lester had suggested they spend the day at a gaudily coloured fairground called *Pleasureland*.

When they arrived at the fairground, Lester

approached a small pink and white booth. He attempted to buy some snacks but the cashier began to give him a lecture.

'Your friends may not be your friends like you think,' a werewolf said, who was wearing a net across his head to hold down a thick comb-over haircut.

'Come again?' Lester asked.

'Oh, yes,' the werewolf said, nodding his head. 'You think they're your friends, but how can you be sure?'

'I see. Ah, can I have that candy floss now?'

'It was two wasn't it?'

'Please. Whenever you're ready.'

The werewolf began to rotate a small machine and he then placed a stick in each of Lester's hands. He then paused and looked at Lester's bald head.

'On the house,' the werewolf said, a friendly smile forming on his face. 'Our kind has to look out for each other, don't we?'

'Yes… of course, we do,' Lester replied, his face one of confused pleasantry. As he walked away, he muttered under his breath: 'The sun always brings them out.' He then walked back to Rita and held out a stick of the fluffy treat for her.

'How about some candy floss?'

'I think I've had enough sugar for one day. You have a sweet tooth don't you?' Rita asked.

'To go with my sweet face.'

'Let's go on the roller-coaster first,' Rita suggested, pointing to a small cart that was zipping along a high peak. It was framed by a burning orange sun.

'Not my thing. But you go on it. I'll wait here and eat my candy floss.'

'Why don't you want to go on the roller-coaster?'

'Because I don't like heights.'

'You're a dragon! How can you not like heights? Surely, you fly in the sky all the time?'

'Not really. Heights give me anxiety. Sometimes I fly, but only short distances and not from too high up.'

'Hmm…' Rita said to herself, mulling over what he had said. She then noticed something to her left. 'Isn't that Donnelly coming out of the ghost train?' she asked.

'Yes,' Lester replied. 'And isn't that a sweet picture?'

Rita began to chuckle at the sight of Donnelly strapped into the grey steel ghost train carriage. The inspector looked like he had been scared to death. When he dismounted the carriage his legs could be seen shaking.

'Well, well. It's Inspector Fearless,' Lester said, and he broke into a fit of laughter.

'I was till I went in there,' Donnelly replied. 'Those ghosts go too far these days. They nearly gave me a heart attack.'

'They probably said the same thing after you left.'

'Funny,' Donnelly said, his face etched with seriousness. 'And what do you want today, laughing boy?'

'Any leads on the burglaries?'

'No. I'm on my day off and thankful for it,' Donnelly said, removing a flat cap from his head and wiping his brow. 'Those two aren't the only crimes in town you know. There's been a spate of antique and jewellery burglaries since then. I'd like to catch the cheeky beggars red-handed. My ears are killing me from all the grief shop owners are giving me. Have you any fresh information?' he asked, his face a sweaty pensive frown.

'Nothing yet,' Lester said. 'Something will turn up when we least expect it.'

'Brilliant detective work! Don't let me keep you,' Donnelly said, rolling his eye. 'I'm off to enjoy the rest of my day, do keep in touch won't you?'

'Yeah, see you later, flat feet. We'll give you a call when we solve the case for you,' Lester said, under his breath.

A used newspaper was floating in the air, and it suddenly landed in front of Lester. *Jade Mask to go on show at the Green Crane Museum* the paper's headline story read.

'Take a look at this,' he said, picking up the crinkled newspaper and turning it to show Rita. 'Donnelly said a lot of jewellery burglaries had taken place.'

'Listen to this part,' said Rita. 'It says "the Green Crane Museum will hold a special party to celebrate the exhibition of the Jade Mask. The party will take place between two pm and eight pm tonight. Guests will be treated to free champagne and food." I'll bet that party will be popular.'

'Oh, it certainly will,' Lester said, and he pointed at the photograph of the Jade Mask. 'Now, if you were stealing jewels, wouldn't this be a nice item to add to your collection?'

'You think they'll try and take it?'

'Yes, and when they do, I'm going to be there to catch them red-handed.'

'Can I come with you?'

'I don't know about that.' Lester suddenly looked deep in thought. 'Okay, you can come. But leave any rough stuff to me.'

'If that's how you want it. But don't go too hard on them, tough guy,' said Rita.

# CHAPTER EIGHTEEN

## Army of Shadows

The simmering heat of the day had faded. As the night took over, it painted the sky black. Only the stars broke through its coating. A gentle wind blew that was neither warm nor cold. There was the odd rumble of thunder, but the sky remained clear.

Lester and Rita were sitting facing the Green Crane Museum. They had set themselves up on the roof of a run-down building on Goodis Street. So far, the only action had been an old beaten-up rubbish truck. It was making its late-night rounds and beeping morosely as it reversed. Lester had watched its flashing amber lights, grateful for some distraction.

So far, Lester and Rita's stakeout had been long and boring. Minutes had painfully turned into hours, and nothing of note had happened. Lester had managed to keep himself busy for most of the night. He had used their stakeout as an excuse to fill his face. So far he had eaten a large bag of salted popcorn, four cheese sandwiches, and some large dates called Medjools.

'I don't know how you sleep at night,' Rita said, as she watched Lester drink coffee out of an enormous flask.

'My conscience is clear, that's how.'

'No, I meant the… forget it. Do you think the thieves will show up tonight?'

'I have a feeling they will, but only after everyone else has left.'

The party's guests came streaming out of the museum just after eight o'clock.

'I think that's the Baron and Delilah,' said Rita.

'Where?'

'Down there. The young woman, dressed in a white ball gown, with a shorter man. I think he's wearing a tuxedo.'

'I can't tell from here, are you sure it's them?'

'I think so,' said Rita. 'Pass me the binoculars.'

'I don't have any.'

'You don't have any! How can you be a private detective with no binoculars?'

'Keep your voice down,' Lester whispered, his face showing traces of guilt. 'I just haven't got round to buying some yet.'

'Honestly! You need to get your act together.'

'I promise I will get some tomorrow; now, keep your eyes peeled.'

Above them, a clap of thunder could be heard and the grey clouds, now turning black, started to pour. Thick, heavy rain spilt down and began to turn the building's roof into a paddling pool.

'Just wonderful, now we're going to get soaked,' said Lester, straightening his bowler hat.

'I've got a small umbrella,' Rita replied, 'It's in my—'

At that moment Lester and Rita were thrown into silence. A hooded figure had landed from above them with a yellow and black striped parachute, right on the building's ledge. They were put in darkness as the parachute dropped gently covering both of them. The hooded figure stood on the building's edge looking down at the museum. He detached the parachute from his back and a sharp clicking sound passed through the air.

'Do you think he saw us?' asked Rita, the weight of the parachute holding her down.

'I don't think so,' said Lester, who was trying to cut through the parachute with his claws. 'He must be skilled to make a landing like that.'

From outside the parachute, they could hear a zip open as the hooded figure reached into a pack slung around his stomach. He pulled out a long metal chain, attached to the end of which was a large hook.

The front door of the museum was being locked for the night by a security guard. He did not look up or even notice the hooded figure staring down at him. On hearing a noise, the guard briefly looked behind him and saw rainwater overflowing from a nearby manhole.

When the guard was out of sight, the hooded figure spun his chain in a circle to gather momentum and let go; the attached hook landed on the edge of the museum's roof.

Lester had managed to cut a hole in the parachute. He watched the hooded figure jump and swing across the gap between the two buildings. 'That chain is too long; he's going to hit the front of the building!' Lester shouted in alarm. He stared in horror waiting for the impact.

Just then, eight feet away from the front door of the museum, the hooded figure let go of the chain and performed a backflip in mid-air, landing squarely on his feet, just one metre from the door. A large puddle of water was flung into the air as his boots made contact.

'Wow!' said Rita amazed. 'He must be an acrobat.'

Down in the street, the hooded figure was staring at the museum's front door. It was made of steel and there were several locks set against it. A bolt of lightning flickered and framed the scene with harsh white light. Pink and green neon lighting flashed, opening up the night further. The large goggles worn by the mysterious figure reflected the light.

'Now we'll see his neatest trick,' said Lester, as he watched with fascination.

The hooded figure removed a long canister from the side of his right leg. Liquid began to pour from one end of it. He proceeded to cover the door from head to foot with the liquid. A scorched hot metal scream came from the door.

'Painfully clever,' said Lester.

'What's he doing?'

'He's using some kind of acid to get through the door. Then he's probably going to steal the Jade Mask. Wait here and don't move. Understood?'

'Yes, I understand,' said Rita. She pulled out her small umbrella, but it was useless against the onslaught of soaking rain.

Lester spread his wings and flew down to the museum. The rain became heavier. A sensor light at the museum door lit him up in red as he landed. He took a deep breath and entered the building where the museum's front door had once stood. The door was now a crumpled steel ruin, smoking from where the acid had burnt through it.

Left out in the cold, Rita Wong shivered.

Inside the museum, amidst the dark shadows, the hooded figure had found the mask. It was locked securely in a glass cabinet in the middle of a roped-off exhibition. The figure ran a hand over the smooth container. He reached into his pocket and pulled out a glass cutter. He paused to look over his shoulder and began to rip into the glass. Behind him, a large painting by the artist Horace

Vernet looked on. It displayed a faded green and brown scene of outlaws being surrounded by Italian troops.

Lester had walked slowly through three rooms trying to spot the thief. The floor lights glowed, with red lights to the left and green to the right. A set of white floor lights pointed ahead with arrows. Lester wondered if they led to the main exhibition room. He decided to follow them and find out.

With his heart beating fast, Lester stood still. His throat was tight, his shoulders tighter. Attempting to tune into the quiet of the museum, he held his breath. His patient silence was rewarded. Hearing a grating noise, he walked towards the sound. He could now see the thief, who was busily working his way into the mask cabinet. He found a light switch on a nearby wall and flicked it on.

'Stop right there!' shouted Lester, pointing at his prey.

The thief looked up and rose to his feet as if to attack. He stepped out of the shadows and into the illumination of a bright floodlight.

Lester saw that the thief was dressed in a red satin cloak. He noticed large reflective eyes looking

129

out from the hood of the cloak. They were as big as oranges but glassy and emotionless. There were no other discernible features except a thin and neutral mouth.

Expecting a violent confrontation, Lester readied himself. Instead of attacking, the thief gave out a metallic groan and grabbed his head. The thief shook his head from left to right as he fell to his knees.

'Are you alright?' Lester asked, disturbed by the thief's sudden agony.

The thief said nothing and pulled something from his face, throwing it into a corner of the room.

'I say! What kind of creature are you?'

Keeping his head down, the thief put one hand in his pocket. He removed a handful of red and green dust which he threw in the dragon's direction. The dust went into Lester's face and he fell to the floor, desperately trying to clear it from his eyes.

'Serves you right for interfering,' the thief said, in a low metallic voice.

Outside, the museum's alarm had been ringing for some time since the break in. Police sirens could be heard by the dozen. The thief looked at the Jade Mask, still encased in glass.

'Drat!' he screeched and ran towards the exit.

Inspector Donnelly was standing in front of the museum. The receding rain had soaked him from head to foot. He was surrounding the building with police officers. He then issued a warning through a loudspeaker.

'Whoever is inside, come out with your hands up!' he shouted. 'It's useless to try and escape; give up now.'

The thief appeared at the door with his hands in the air.

'Arrest that man,' Donnelly said, aiming a torch at the thief.

Five of his best police officers walked over with handcuffs to take the thief into custody. Before they got near him there was a death whistle. The sound was excruciating to the police officers' ears. They desperately looked around trying to find the source of the painful hissing.

The boots the hooded figure was wearing had released a mixture of smoke and powder. The whistle of the boots gave way to a whooshing noise as the smoke became thicker. No one was able to see anything for the next few minutes.

When the air had finally cleared, the thief had vanished. 'I don't believe this,' Donnelly said, stamping his foot on the ground. 'Jimmy, get in there and find out what he's taken!'

Minutes later, the small chubby policeman came out of the museum. 'I don't think he's taken anything, boss. But we found a dragon inside. Maybe he's an accomplice?'

'Or maybe he's a bumbling know-it-all,' Donnelly said, under his breath. 'Jimmy, cordon off Goodis and Grafton Street. Don't let anyone leave the area.'

'My word it's hot in here,' Lester said, as he wiped the coloured dust from his eyes.

'Good evening, I think I just met a friend of yours,' said Donnelly, looking down at the dragon sprawled across the floor.

'He was a thief after the Jade Mask,' said Lester, standing up and pointing at the badly damaged glass cabinet.

'Stone the crows! Why didn't you grab hold of him?'

'That was rather difficult as he threw dust at me. Although it's out of my eyes now. I'm fine by the way.'

'You're lucky our unwelcome guest didn't hurt you more severely.'

Lester stood up and brushed the dust off his hat. He then noticed something across the room that was glinting under the lights. He strode over to the corner and picked up the object.

'That explains it,' he said.

'Explains what?'

'When I walked in, the thief was trying to break into the cabinet. I decided to switch on the lights to surprise him. When I did, he hollered in pain and pulled this off his face.' Lester passed what looked like a pair of binoculars to the inspector.

'What are they?'

'Night vision goggles: they amplify light so you can see things in the dark. If you put them on under bright lights the effect is certainly painful.'

'Is that right?' said Donnelly, running a hand through his bushy brown hair. 'Well, no matter what he brought with him, he's nothing but a common thief. We'll find him.'

'This isn't just a common thief.'

'Why isn't he?'

'Common thieves don't swing on buildings, perform gymnastics in mid-air, open steel doors with acid, and they certainly can't afford expensive night vision goggles.'

'I think you have a point there,' Donnelly conceded, folding his arms across his chest. 'Right then, let's set up a perimeter. I'll ask forensics to dust for prints. Come on, let's leave them to it.'

As Lester walked out of the museum, he saw Rita waving at him from behind a police barrier. She looked soaked to the bone and tired. Her skin appeared ice-blue from the police car lights around her. She was also out of breath.

'Are you alright?' asked Lester.

'It took me a while to get down all the stairs in the building across the street,' said Rita. 'Did they escape with the Jade Mask?'

'No,' replied Donnelly. 'Your friend here decided to be a hero.'

'Did this hero save the Jade Mask from theft?' asked a dwarf who was carrying several cameras.

'Er, well, he did save the mask but I don't know if he's a—' Donnelly was curtly interrupted by the dwarf, who turned round to a gathering throng of news reporters.

'We've got ourselves a hero!' the dwarf declared with all his might. 'My name is Spike Mitchell, chief reporter for the *Daily Dwarf Chronicle*. How did you stop him?'

'Who?' asked Lester, stunned by the use of the word *hero*.

'The mask thief!' said Spike, as a hot flashbulb on his camera popped and nearly blinded Lester.

'I'll have no eyeballs left if this carries on!' Lester complained, rubbing his eyes.

Spike Mitchell reached for another camera slung around his neck and took a photograph of Rita. He then pulled a notepad from the pocket of his grey flannel suit.

Spike's small hazel eyes levelled on Lester.

'Come on hero,' he bellowed. 'Tell us everything.'

'I don't know where to begin.'

'You can start with your name!'

'His name is Lester and he's a private detective,' said Rita.

'Private detective, eh?' Spike replied, one of his eyebrows rising.

Lester merely nodded in agreement. He was in shock from the number of reporters surrounding him and taking his photograph.

'How did you know a crime was going to be committed?' said Spike to Rita.

'We didn't really, to be honest. Lester had a hunch that the thieves he was after would try and steal the mask.'

'Fantastic,' said Spike, scribbling wildly in his notepad. 'The dragon acted on a hunch!'

'What did the thief look like?' another reporter asked.

'We didn't get a proper look at him,' Lester said, now getting over his initial shock.

'He was about five feet high and wore a cloak,' said Rita.

Lester was becoming rather worried. If the thief found out anything about him, he might come after him to get his revenge.

'That's probably enough for now,' he said to the crowd.

'Come on!' Spike demanded. 'One more question!' And the reporters behind him began to grumble in agreement.

'Just one more,' Lester agreed.

'Were you already on a case working for someone?'

'I don't reveal the names of my clients to—'

'He's looking for Mr Que's stolen antique swords,' Rita said.

Lester glanced at Rita as if to say 'better not to reveal anything else'. He saw Rita nod and draw a finger across her mouth.

As they walked away from the crime scene, Lester could hear Spike shouting out behind him.

'This is going to make great copy! Famous private detective foils mask thief.'

From out of the large crowd, now surrounding the museum, a familiar figure appeared. She leaned forward and tapped Lester on the shoulder.

'Congratulations, Lester. I overheard that reporter say you stopped a burglary tonight.' The voice belonged to Delilah Chang, who was wearing a red ball gown.

'Not quite… actually, yes I did.'

Rita coughed loudly.

'Better get some medicine for that,' said Lester and turned back to Delilah. 'Say, are you—'

Rita coughed twice more and looked up with a frown on her face.

'What's up with you?'

'Shouldn't you be taking me home?' she said, tapping her watch with two fingers.

'Good point.'

'May I buy you a drink?' Delilah asked Lester, brushing a curtain of brown hair away from her right eye.

'No, I mean yes.'

'My father owns a nightclub; we can meet there.'

'Excuse me,' Rita said, looking up at Lester.

'I need to drop my partner off at home first.'

'Of course,' Delilah replied, giving him a card with the club's address printed on it. 'We can meet there round about midnight.'

'We shall,' said Lester, smiling to himself and treating the small card as if it was made of gold.

Lester and Rita walked away. Delilah turned to walk east on York Street, towards a large marine-blue limousine. At her side, a man wearing a chauffeur's hat held a red umbrella over her head.

When Delilah was some distance away, Rita turned to Lester: 'Just be careful she's not leading you into a trap. Don't you find it a little strange how she got to the scene of the crime so quickly?'

'Yes, I do. It was good timing on her part wasn't it?'

'Crackerjack timing. There is something wrong here.'

'I think so too,' Lester replied, 'I haven't been on a date in ten years. I'd better go home and have a bath.'

'No, I mean wrong and dangerous.'

# CHAPTER NINETEEN

## The Electric Witness

It was under the giant redwood tree on Chester Avenue that Ermington Snyde realised he was being followed. He could detect the sound of footsteps in a mist which smelt of petrol fumes. His house was only a ten-minute walk away, but he slowed his pace deliberately. His right hand slipped into his inside jacket pocket. There his fingers grasped for a smooth black dagger.

'There is no need for that, Snyde,' said a low measured voice coming from the other side of the tree.

Ermington stepped back under the glare of a copper

streetlight. His immaculate smooth suit absorbed the cool night breeze. His eyes narrowed, and he readied himself for a skirmish.

From behind the tree, a tall teddy bear stepped out into the glare of the streetlight. His face, mottled and darker than the red-brown tree bark, displayed no emotion.

'Long time no see, Fred,' Ermington said, lowering himself into a deep bow.

The teddy bear dipped his head to acknowledge the bow.

'I see you are enjoying freedom.'

'Just a simple night walk,' Ermington replied.

'Life is an enjoyment of simple moments,' observed Fred, straightening his red bow tie. He then sniffed a scarlet lily flower in the buttonhole of his jacket.

Ermington's eyes took in the quality of the teddy bear's suit. It was checked and glossy. It gave its wearer a polished appearance.

'By the cut of your cloth, it seems you've been enjoying life more than I.'

'That is true, Snyde. Although I do not carry the burden of having been publicly shamed.'

'No, you certainly do not. Did it cost you a pretty penny to do that to me?' Ermington asked, his fingers once again creeping towards his dagger.

'I am merely a servant, not the writer of cheques,' Fred said. He then pointed to several figures behind Ermington. 'But I will pay you in blood if you remove that weapon from your pocket.'

Looking behind him, Ermington saw five figures walking along the tarmac pavement towards them. They were all well-dressed in black suits, and the sound of their steps grew louder in the night. He turned back to look at their leader, his eyebrows tensed and raised together.

'I see you're not lonely tonight,' said Ermington.

'Quite the contrary. But I am only here to deliver a message.'

'Please inform me. I am a willing recipient.'

'The lady still wants the ring returned to her. And you still owe her the life of her man.'

'That was a hundred years ago or more!' Ermington protested, rubbing the back of his neck. 'I told you the detective killed him. I cannot be held responsible—'

'Silence!' Fred commanded. 'You will find the ring for the lady. Then you will kill whoever the current owner is. Once that message has been delivered, your debt will be paid.'

'It could be anywhere. We've been looking for it for over a century.'

'Perhaps you know where it is already. You never could tell the truth, Snyde. With your lies, I imagine you have known the owner all this time.'

'I am a reformed character, and more than willing to help.'

'Then you should start looking for the ring. Now.'

'I gave the lady everything she asked for in the past. Is this to be one of many more undertakings?'

'Once the ring is back on her finger, then we will see,' Fred replied, and one corner of his mouth turned up. The stitching in his smile became tight. 'Now I bid you goodnight, Snyde.' As the teddy bear turned, Ermington saw a multitude of black electric cables wired into the back of Fred's head. In the middle of his back was an oily plug socket.

Ermington crossed over to the other side of the avenue. After a minute, he turned to look over his shoulder. Fred had vanished into the mist, taking his followers with him.

Letting out a deep breath, Ermington considered

the position he was in. He had been foolish to think that the lady would ever let him go free. To owe her a debt was akin to a life sentence of servitude. Her dainty walk and indifferent face were in stark contrast to her cold vindictiveness.

In the lonely night of Neon City, Ermington felt a sense of powerlessness. He had few followers and certainly not the thousands that the lady commanded. He now had to obey his former employer's orders for the time being. There was also the humiliation of bowing to all who served her. He hoped that was a temporary measure.

Now, Ermington would have to work harder than ever. His only alternative was to retire and hide in the shadows. That was simply impossible.

# CHAPTER TWENTY

## Gambling House

Lester arrived thirty minutes early at a nightclub called *The Cabinet*. He had hoped to look around the club before Delilah arrived. He wanted to familiarise himself with it and not appear like a fish out of water. Moving swiftly, he buttoned up his coat in the damp night air.

As Lester reached the end of Shadow Street, he saw a large unfriendly troll guarding the club's door. The troll was dressed in a black suit and he approached Lester quickly.

'Are you going somewhere, buddy?' he asked, a

damaged street light flickering against his sandpaper skin.

'I've been invited here by Delilah Chang,' Lester said, removing his bowler hat.

The troll went silent, then stepped closer. He carried the scent of sweat and the dark demeanour of a hard life. He was at least a foot taller than Lester and hovered over him. 'You've been invited have you?' he said, pulling a piece of paper from his pocket. 'What's your name?' he asked, unfolding his list.

'Lester Thyme.'

'I see your name down on my list. You've not come here to cause trouble have you?'

'Certainly not.'

'Then you can enter and enjoy yourself. Take care.'

Lester smiled and nodded. He felt slightly confused by the exchange but also more cautious as a result of it.

Through the door was a small lobby with six chrome and silver chairs. On the wall above them was a painting of a glamorous woman standing next to a lion. Across from the picture was a walnut bookcase designed to look like a skyscraper. A waitress was serving coffee to a wizard. A thick waft of tobacco smoke ran through the lobby from a hookah pipe the wizard was using. Neither the waitress nor the wizard looked at Lester. It made him feel unwelcome and, not liking the smell of tobacco smoke, he moved on.

Leaving the lobby area through a set of doors decorated with gold leaf, Lester found himself in a large casino with slot machines and gaming tables. In front of him was a carnival of high-stakes gambling, flashing lights, and a kaleidoscope of rousing colours. The view was one of financial hazard and the seductive magnetism of being among people who have money to burn.

He was brought out of his thoughts by a nearby porter.

'May I take your coat, sir?'

'Please, if you don't mind,' Lester replied, feeling as if he had just woken from a gaudy dream. 'Do you know a lady called Delilah Chang?'

'Indeed I do, sir. She's been here for some time. If you'll follow me, I'll take you to her.'

As he trailed the porter, Lester felt the thick carpet beneath his feet. It was like walking on a gentle bed of rose petals and must have cost a fortune. It was in a design of stylised yellow flowers.

A green and white corridor led away from the casino, at the end of which was a gold door studded with pearls. The porter opened it and gestured for Lester to step through it.

'She's just in here, sir,' he said, bowing deeply.

As Lester stepped through the door, he heard the ecstatic chants of people having a good time. They were seated around glass tables that contained a selection of desserts from around the world. There were Black Forest cherry cakes from Germany, deep-fried sweets from India, apple pies from America, raspberry ice creams from Italy, and hot doughnuts from Peru.

At the end of the room, lit with peach lighting by a chrome chandelier, a pianist let his fingers dance over the keys. Standing at his side was Delilah Chang. She had since changed outfits. Now she was wearing a long blue sequined dress with a gem studded bronze head cap. Around her neck was a simple gold chain. She was holding a silk parasol above her head in one hand, and a mother of pearl fan in the other. She stood on an apple-wood stage framed by blue drapes that hung down to the floor. Singing along with the piano music, her playful husky voice instantly put Lester at ease:

He opened the door with a swaggering kick,
While she was decorating with a lipstick,
She was standing by the bar with a drink
in hand,
Her Autumn toned hair held back by a
band,
When in comes Mr Confidence Trick.

She's no time for a dumb sidekick,
His kind knows what makes a woman tick,
That man dared to create a spin,
He was not handsome, he was not thin,
He said "Hello" with a cautious grin,
And told her his name was Mr Confidence
Trick.

Eyes gathered to witness their conception,
A large male audience suggested deception,
They could not understand or comprehend
the attraction,
"She could do better" was their reaction,
Their affair needs no arithmetic,
They fell in love, real double-quick,
The private eye who fell from grace,

*A femme fatale with a beautiful face,*
*Yet they have knowing smiles,*
*For they have something much worthwhile,*
*They're more tactile than a house brick,*
*They're Mr and Mrs Confidence Trick.*


As she brought the song to an end, everyone rose to their feet and applauded. Delilah walked over to Lester's table, much to the envy of many onlookers.

'Was that in tune?'

'The voices of angels always are,' Lester replied.

'Thank you. You look good in here, almost comfortable.'

'I'm trying my best, but it's all an act.'

'I don't doubt it,' Delilah said, placing her fan and parasol on the table. 'Don't you often walk the mean streets at night?'

'My opening times are usually during the day.'

'I hope I'm not keeping you up?'

'I'm a big boy. I'll be safe walking home on my own.'

'Better be sure, there's a full moon tonight.'

'I don't mind as long as it makes the stars sparkle.'

'My, my, a private detective and a poet. Any more strings to your bow?'

'No, but I listen good and learn quickly.'

'That's an admirable quality in a dangerous city,' she said, sipping from a glass of water. 'Now for your drink, do you want trouble or safe?' she asked, as a waiter stood over their table.

'I'll play it safe with a calm morning drink of coffee.'

'I'll walk on the wild side if you don't mind. I'll take a Neon City Swing,' she said to the waiter. 'Tell me, Lester,' she said, opening her left hand to show the palm. 'How long can you keep this up?'

'Excuse me?'

'Come on, this detective act of yours won't wash.'

'It's clean and on the level.'

'I hope so. I'd hate to see someone nice get hurt.'

'Me, nice?'

'You, nice,' Delilah said, pointing at him. 'You look green, and maybe soft inside like a banana.'

'Just because my face is pretty and my hands are smooth doesn't mean I can't do a day's work.'

'I'll take your word for it. Is a tough guy like you in a lot of demand?'

'Diamonds are always popular because they're durable and look good.'

'Is that a fact? Your latest case… how much is your retainer, may I ask?'

'Seventy thousand yen,' Lester bragged.

'If you were to drop that case, my father could pay you a retainer of at least two hundred thousand yen.'

'Two hundred thousand!'

'Yes, plus a bonus upon completion,' she added, removing some ice cubes from her drink.

'You seem to know a lot about your father's business?'

'I don't just help him with antiques.'

Lester thought long and hard about the offer. Two hundred thousand yen meant he would be able to fix his house up, buy more clothes, and treat himself to drinks more often.

'I can't. I need to attend to Mr Que's case first,' he said, apologising. 'I make it a rule never to disappoint a client. I've my reputation to think of.'

'Such a shame,' Delilah replied. 'But perhaps we can do business in the future.'

'I'd certainly like that.'

When they finished their drinks, the waiter brought

a receipt for Delilah to sign. A copy was left on the table. As Lester helped Delilah put on her coat, he picked up the black silk receipt and put it into his wallet as a memento.

As they left the restaurant, Lester saw a bulb flash in his face followed by a loud popping sound.

'My eyes!' Lester shrieked. 'If he does that again, I'm taking legal action.'

To the side of the restaurant doorway, Spike Mitchell the reporter smiled and held up two more cameras.

'Is this your lovely girlfriend, Lester?' he asked, the bulbs on his cameras popping in sync.

'No, she's a friend, thank you. And would you please stop doing that?'

'Miss, how does it feel to go out with a hero?'

'My name is Delilah.' And with that, she pushed Spike's cameras away from her.

'As in Delilah Chang? So that's who Lester is working for!'

'Ignore him,' Lester said, walking away from Spike.

Delilah nodded and reached into her handbag. She passed Lester a pair of gold hinged sunglasses with brown hexagonal lenses. 'I thought all you private eyes carried these?' she said.

Lester smiled and accepted the sunglasses. 'To tell you the truth, I never thought anyone would want to take my picture,' he replied.

'Maybe it's because you've been such a busy bee lately?'

'Perhaps. I suppose I should be getting back to the beehive. Will you be alright?'

'Oh, don't worry about that. My driver will take me home. Listen, Lester… call me sometime,' she said, tapping his upper arm with her warm hand. 'It's nice to be around someone exciting for a change.'

Delilah leaned against Lester and kissed him softly on the cheek. He felt a funny sensation in his stomach after the kiss, as if something had changed. He walked away from the club, his frame lit up by a pink floodlight. He had a long walk ahead of him, but he was not daunted. When he reached the end of the street, Lester Thyme turned a corner.

# CHAPTER TWENTY-ONE

## The Neon Express

The palace on wheels accelerated into the night's rain. A beast of a train, it defied the cold downpour. The rain tried its best, but could not penetrate the silver carriages. Beneath them, the copper wheels shook the rails.

Proudly efficient, the hard exterior of the train concealed its inner finery. Within its ten carriages, it carried furnishings fit for royalty. A blood-red carpet guarded every floor, and scarlet curtains defended every window. Emerald-green velvet chairs protected each passenger, while teak tables kept their possessions in order.

High-end air conditioning kept the room temperature at twenty-two degrees throughout the train. It also carried the fragrant aromas of coffee, chocolate, and cinnamon. The latter scent was emanating from a tray of crisp glazed Danish pastries. They were carried from carriage to carriage by a car attendant wearing a pink silk dress.

When she reached compartment thirteen, the Cambodian car attendant knocked three times on the walnut door. Again there was no answer from within. The shiny wooden door had also remained closed when she had tried to serve dinner earlier in the evening. She carefully held the tray of pastries with her left hand. With her right hand, she put a stray lock of her glossy black hair back in place. Then she straightened her dress and moved on to the next compartment.

Inside compartment thirteen a metallic smell of oil swirled in the air.

Laid out on a large oak table were the crude components of a disassembled instrument. Among them was also a twenty-five-centimetre steel wand decorated at one end with a small double-edged battle-axe.

On either side of the table were large green leather armchairs. The occupant of one was male and five feet in height. Strapped to his face was a mask in the design of a frog's face. The overly large metal mask was shiny and green in colour. Through two eye holes, the cautious grey eyes of a man looked out. They were staring at a slender blonde woman. She appeared to be on edge, and she ran her hand across her forehead, then onto her smooth cheek.

'You worry too much,' the man said, as he began to assemble the components of a weapon.

'Perhaps. I still don't understand why we're doing this, Marvin.'

'We're for hire,' he replied. 'So we do whatever we're asked. Try to focus more, Kitty.'

The woman nodded. Behind her, and visible through the carriage window, was a trail of storm damage from the month before. Shattered apple trees leaned forward and threatened to crush the white roses beneath them. The view was one of chaos. A similar view was soon to be seen throughout the interior of the train.

There was a loud click as Marvin finished assembling the object. His large fat paw of a hand passed Kitty a small pearl-handled silver wand.

'Be careful with it,' he said, before picking up his steel wand and filling the archaic weapon with blue dust from a tatty cloth bag.

Kitty straightened up in her chair and said: 'Our seat tickets cost more than this job will make us. What's the point of a robbery if you don't make a profit?'

The frog mask rotated to the right like the hour hand on a clock face.

'Someone took something a long time ago. That thing cost a king his life. If we find someone carrying it on this train... then they die too,' Marvin said, flicking the steel wand with his index finger. 'Revenge is worth more than money. Bear that in mind, and next time you won't need to ask so many questions.'

Kitty nodded her head.

'The train is twenty minutes from the centre of Neon City,' Marvin announced. 'We're running parallel with Entrance Road,' he added, checking his frog mask was secure. 'Now put your mask on and follow my lead.'

161

Kitty did as she was told. From out of a small wooden box, she removed an old World War II gas mask. She carefully fitted it to her delicate face. When finished, she gave Marvin a thumbs-up sign.

Looking down at his watch, Marvin noticed the time was twenty-two minutes past two in the morning. He gripped the smooth steel wand in his right hand and rose from his chair.

As the car attendant glided through the train, she saw the door to compartment thirteen finally open. She saw two figures, in orange boiler suits, emerge. Both of them wore bizarre disguises and brandished weapons in their hands. Before she could turn and run for help, a steady feminine New York accent stopped her in her tracks.

'Take a seat lady,' the voice commanded. The mouth that had spoken was covered again as the gas mask was moved back into position.

Then the frog face started to talk. 'We mean no one any harm. You are going to help us, young lady,' the frog said in a low guttural American accent. 'I want you to walk in front of us. Tell the passengers we only want their rings. We don't need any other jewellery or cash. Rings only. Do you understand?'

The Cambodian lady nodded. 'I understand perfectly,' she replied.

'Good,' the frog said. 'In ten minutes this will all be over. Then everyone on board can have some coffee and a Danish. Then they can get back to being rich and important,' he growled, the soft gold lighting framing his cold eyes.

# CHAPTER TWENTY-TWO

## Coffee in the Moonlight

The night wind carried an oppressive chill. Lester Thyme pulled his coat to and decided to take a tram home. He walked along Glass Street and then crossed over to York Street. The streetlights lit up the empty pavement, and nothing stirred anywhere.

Cut into the corner of York Street, a coffee shop called the *Moonlight* was bustling. Lester stopped for a moment to look at its patrons. His tired mind asked who was up at such a late hour.

The front of the shop was encased in square plate glass. Green light flooded the exterior of the building, while gentle candlelight kept the interior visible. Inside, a triangular mahogany counter was covered with salt and sugar shakers. Behind it, in a white uniform, a witch scrambled to refill coffee cups.

Lester leaned forward and squinted his eyes. At one end of the counter, he could see Inspector Donnelly. He was sitting on a stool and had wrapped himself in a grey overcoat. He had placed his flat cap on the counter. He was looking dejected and was sipping a dun-coloured liquid from a tall glass.

Grabbing the chrome door lever, Lester walked into the *Moonlight*.

'Are you alright, Donnelly?' he asked.

The inspector looked up. His large eye, reflecting candlelight, appeared bloodshot and sombre.

'Here's to redundancy,' he said, lifting the thick glass to his even thicker lips.

'That stuff won't help,' Lester replied, and he dropped down into the stool next to Donnelly. A fine mist of espresso coffee blew between them, the bitter Colombian fumes reaching for the ceiling.

'I'm not sure much will help me, Mr Lester. There was a robbery thirty minutes ago on the Neon Express. A train full of very important people. All of whom are now missing rings on their fingers. I just received a call from the mayor about it.'

'I bet he wasn't a happy bunny.'

'No he wasn't, and it's not even Easter. He's given me two weeks to get the jewellery back or else. Can you imagine how it feels to be in a position like that?'

'Actually, I might have an idea.'

'Maybe you do,' Donnelly replied. He began to massage the inside of his left palm with a thumb. 'Life is such a tightrope at times,' he said. 'No matter how hard you work, something always knocks you back.' He let out a breath and shook his head from left to right. 'There are people in this city whose hourly wage is not enough to buy two cups of coffee.'

'I suppose that's life,' Lester replied. 'Some get to stand in the middle of the stadium, while others can't even get in the car park.'

Donnelly moved closer to Lester. His forehead dipped slightly as he began to whisper. 'You can see the temptation of it, can't you?'

'Not quite. Why don't you explain?'

'You know. Working for the other side. The bad guys. I bet they don't threaten pension pots.'

'I imagine they threaten more important things.'

'Possibly,' Donnelly said, raising his glass to the light. 'Here's to the soldiers who are always needed,' he proposed.

'Are you drunk?'

'On this stuff?' Donnelly replied, looking at his glass. 'It's just Oolong Tea.'

'Oh, I see... was anything else stolen from this train you mentioned?'

'Nothing.'

'They just took the rings?'

'Yes, indeed they did. And they were not armed with swords before you ask. But they did ignore a large number of French francs the train was carrying. They simply focused on stealing every ring they could get their sticky fingers on.'

'I wonder,' Lester said, holding his hand up to summon the witch, 'if perhaps our robber friends are strictly Neon City natives.'

'How so?' Donnelly asked, leaning the right side of his face against his hand.

'They've stolen stuff they can fence here. They've no interest in real money that can be used in the human world. It's as if they're stealing to order. Which suggests one person is in charge of them.'

'I doubt they vote on the crimes.'

Lester nodded as the witch filled a ceramic cup with coffee for him. 'Donnelly, what if all this is a smokescreen?'

'Meaning what?'

'Distraction. To divert attention from something far bigger and more important.'

'You think deep thoughts. But they should not be ignored,' Donnelly, said polishing off the rest of his tea with a large gulp.

The glass window of the *Moonlight* began to rhythmically thump with a downpour of heavy rain. Lester looked through the glass into the empty street behind it. The pavement, streaked with green light, began to glisten.

'I wonder how this city got to be so rotten,' he said.

'It's not so bad,' Donnelly replied, putting his flat cap onto his round head. 'And it can be cleaned up anytime.' He rose to his feet and turned to nod before leaving.

'Welcome to the war, Mr Lester,' he said and stepped into the storm outside.

# CHAPTER TWENTY-THREE

## Criss Cross

When Donnelly walked along Sequin Street, the sky was at peace. The wind and rain had called it quits, the vicious storm passing away. Turning east, Donnelly crossed Clinton Avenue.

Lowering his bowler hat, Lester Thyme followed in the pooled yellow-sapphire lighting of the pavement lamps. He kept his head down and kept sight of Donnelly in his peripheral vision.

They were both heading towards a run-down industrial area that at one time had swarmed with shipbuilders. There was still the odd furnace glowing in the night, a silky rattle and hum echoing from its tapestry of orange heat.

Donnelly passed through the green-lit Neon City train station. He placed a small number of coins in a bowl held by a beggar sitting near the ticket office. Lester expected him to inspect the Neon Express. Instead, Donnelly looked over his shoulder, then shuffled out of the station without stopping. He continued walking, passing along the West India Dock Road. At Fourth Street, he stopped to buy a newspaper.

Hanging back, Lester Thyme leaned into the side of a large billboard advertising red apricots. Behind him, he saw an out-of-shape freight train wrestling with its load. It passed through, whistling in discomfort. The train initially struggled with its new duty of carrying recycled aluminium. As it gathered pace, it seemed to adapt and survived a narrow bend on the way out of the city.

Ahead, Lester saw a news vendor nod at Donnelly and place something into the middle of a newspaper. Donnelly kept looking anxiously over his shoulder. He paid the vendor and continued his walk.

In an attempt to move more smoothly and more

quietly, Lester Thyme opened his coat. His shirt was thin and a night breeze chilled his chest. He wondered what Donnelly was nervous about, and more importantly what he was carrying in his newspaper. He was sure he had seen the inspector quickly eat half a packet of mints too.

'What on earth is he up to?' Lester said quietly under his breath. He decided to continue his pursuit. Donnelly was making a right turn onto the rubbish-lined Third Street. He followed it as it connected with Hill Street. Holding back, Lester slowed to a stop. He let the inspector get ahead of him, and tried to keep calm. Losing Donnelly in a giant metropolis would be easy, but getting too close would be costly.

As Hill Street dipped down, the rainwater cascaded over the pavement and into the gutters. Lester kept a steady pace. His mind raced at the possibility of what Donnelly was up to. Had he got involved with organised crime and betrayed the police force? Or maybe he was just going home? Either way, Lester was going to find out.

As Hill Street joined Franklin Square, Donnelly stopped in his tracks and then darted down a small alleyway. When Lester arrived at the square, he looked around for the inspector. He wondered if he had been made, and stepped away from the glare of a shop front. He squeezed himself into a doorway, and his eyes scanned the view from left to right. It occurred to him that he had no weapon, and he wondered if Donnelly was armed.

Across the square, in front of a bank, a small crowd was gathering. Sensing danger, Lester stepped out of the doorway and into the filthy alleyway. He crouched down on his knees and smelt an overpowering stench of grime. At the end of the alleyway was a set of steel steps connecting to an external staircase. In the moonlight, he caught sight of Donnelly ascending the staircase. Once again he was glancing over his shoulder as if looking for someone tailing him.

Lester walked to the end of the alleyway, and around hot steam blowing out of a manhole cover. He gripped the cold staircase and slowly walked up, one step at a time. Flakes of rust broke away every time his feet made contact. From what he could see, it appeared Donnelly was heading for the roof.

At the top step of the staircase, Lester peered over the edge of the building. He saw no sign of Donnelly. So, he decided to spring onto the roof. At his side, a red neon sign advertising milk throbbed rapidly. On the west corner of the building was another connecting staircase which Donnelly was descending. He seemed to be heading back to Franklin Square.

To make up for the lost time, Lester opened his wings and flew down to a dark alley. As he got closer to the ground, he realised his mistake. He hit two bins and collapsed face down in the alley. The resulting noise brought Donnelly running to him.

Lester pushed himself up onto his feet. He had landed chest down in a large pile of something left behind by a unicorn. His immaculate white shirt was now stained with every colour of the rainbow.

'Just wonderful,' he said, shaking his head and wondering how he could have been so clumsy.

'Why it's Mr Lester,' said Mr Donnelly, who was accompanied by a woman in her thirties. She wore a thick brown artificial fur coat, black high heels, and a red beret. Looking Lester over, she turned to Donnelly.

'Do you know this guy?' she asked.

'Indeed I do. Normally he doesn't look or smell so bad. Well, Mr Lester. What's a dandy like you doing down an alley, covered in unicorn poo?'

'It's not how it looks. Honest.'

'I should hope not,' Donnelly's companion said, holding a blue silk handkerchief over her nose.

'I'm sure he has a good explanation, Freda.'

'Ah, well… I suppose I should be honest,' Lester said. 'I was following you, Donnelly. I wondered what you might do about the train robbery. I also wondered if there could be someone following you.'

'Oh, right,' the inspector said. 'You mean you're my back-up man, is that it?'

'In a sense,' Lester said and nodded his head.

'I wasn't up to much other than taking Freda here for an early breakfast. It's gotten difficult to see each other. I've been so busy of late.'

'I can imagine,' Lester said. Without thinking he blurted out a question: 'What's in the middle of your newspaper?'

Freda turned with a look of suspicion on her broad face: 'Well, what is in the newspaper?' she asked.

Donnelly suddenly looked embarrassed. He took out the paper from under his arm. Unrolling it, he revealed a lilac-coloured flower. 'It's a bee orchid I managed to get hold of. It's for you. It was to celebrate our anniversary.'

'Oh, it's lovely,' Freda said, taking the orchid from him and smiling.

'I'm glad you like it,' said Donnelly waving a hand at Lester. 'Now I think we should get our gooseberry a taxi.'

The three of them walked over to the other side of Franklin Square. As they got there a crowd approached. Leading the crowd was a werewolf. Lester could see that he had a bald head with long hair on both sides hanging over his ears. He also had the strange feeling he had met the werewolf somewhere before.

The crowd behind him wore matching T-shirts which spelt out *Baldness Acceptance Movement*. The werewolf pointed to Donnelly and turned to address the crowd. 'Here's another one!' he shouted. 'Why are you hiding under that wig?' he demanded, turning to look at Donnelly as if he were public enemy number one.

'It's not a wig,' Donnelly said, in a calm tone.

'You big fat liar!' the werewolf screamed, becoming more animated. 'Don't be a coward and admit you're bald.'

'But it's my own hair,' Donnelly replied. 'I promise you—'

Before Donnelly could try to reason with the increasingly hostile crowd, the werewolf put a loudspeaker to his mouth. 'Get woke up and get your wig off!' he shouted at Donnelly. Behind him, his twenty acolytes also pointed their fingers at Donnelly, and shouted together: 'GET WOKE UP AND GET YOUR WIG OFF!'

Stepping backwards, Donnelly made one last attempt to placate them. 'But it's all my own hair. Now return to your homes,' he ordered. When the crowd continued to advance forwards, he reached into his jacket.

'Don't do that,' Lester said, and he touched Donnelly's upper arm.

'I was only going to show them my police badge,' the inspector whispered.

'It's not you they're angry with, let it go. What do you say I give you a lift somewhere?'

'I think that's a good idea,' Freda said, and she took Donnelly's hand as the three of them jumped into a taxi. Behind the taxi, the ugly crowd surged and chanted 'GET YOUR WIG OFF!'

The taxi driver, a dark-brown-eyed elf sporting a blond Mohican, looked in his rear-view mirror and said drily: 'You three should be more careful. All the undead come out at night: ghosts, mummies, vampires, werewolves, zombies, and narcissists. I take them to their castles, I take them to their therapist's office… I don't care.' He then put his foot on the accelerator, whisking them through the steam-hissing streets.

# CHAPTER TWENTY-FOUR

## The Night Holds Terror

At one hundred and twenty-three Main Street, Rita Wong sat with her mother at a white faux marble table. The sun was setting early in Morecambe. The sunset was framed by a pair of purple polyester curtains hanging in a tired kitchen.

Rita had not heard from Lester Thyme all day and she was beginning to worry about him. Now it was six o'clock in the evening.

'You seem on edge. What's the matter with you?'

'Nothing, mother.'

'All you've done for the past few hours is sit there looking worried. Are you expecting a phone call?'

'No. My phone. It wouldn't respond before, but now it's working,' Rita replied, putting the phone away to let her mother know she had her full attention.

'I've been meaning to speak to you about that phone and your computer. I think you're spending too much time on both of them. If you went out more or joined a club you'd have more friends here. It's all well and good having friends on the internet, but real life is more important than that.'

Her mother pushed her square spectacles back and ran a hand through her black-bobbed hair. She took a moment to pause and lowered her voice.

'I know it's been hard for you here, Rita. And I can understand if you feel powerless about what happened in Hong Kong. But that doesn't mean you should live in your head. Since we got here, all you do is daydream and hardly eat anything. You have to give this place a chance. It will take time to adjust, and you'll need to keep an open mind. But I'm sure you can manage it. I think we should talk about it over a cup of tea. Why don't you get some fresh air first? Take a walk to the shop. Get us some milk and a packet of those crumpets I like.'

'Yes, mother,' Rita said dutifully. As agreed, she walked down Vine Street to the shop. On her way home, she had the unnerving feeling she was being watched. Above her, there was a bang from a streetlight followed by a crackle and a hiss. The bulb went out as did every light in the street. She was left in darkness.

Faced with the raw pitch black of the world, all the dogs in the street began to howl together. They then crouched in the smooth black tourmaline of the shadows, trying to hide. Rita looked around for the comforting sign of another person or even a passing car, but there were none. The sky, dark but tinged with red, was also empty.

As she speed-walked home, Rita could smell an exotic perfume. It was initially sweet in smell like flowers, but it also gave off a scent of copper.

As she came to a stop, Rita looked over her shoulder. The night was darker now and a full moon hung in the sky. The cracked grey paving slabs seemed empty enough but the trees? There was something not quite right about the grey poplar trees in the street.

In the moonlight, the branches of the trees looked like the bones of deformed monsters. Stripped off their leaves by the hard winter, the trees were stark and moved unevenly in the bitterly cold wind.

Rita resumed her walk home. It was when she was within ten feet of her house that she heard someone whispering.

'Did you find your friend?' a soft and caressing voice asked.

The voice had come from behind her, but when she turned around there was no one there.

'No,' the voice whispered again. 'I'm up here.'

Nervously, Rita lifted her head.

Within the branches of a redwood tree, a black silk scarf rippled in the wind. It was coiled around the neck of Kim Park who was sitting delicately on a tree branch. Rita marvelled at her sense of balance and noticed Kim looked different than the last time she had seen her.

Although still beautiful, Kim seemed younger. Her eyes, once dark with cynicism, now looked bright and sparkled. From a distance, they glowed crimson red. The overall impression given to Rita was that Kim had satisfied some dark yearning within.

'Yes, I have seen him, thank you,' Rita said, and she began to sense mortal danger. With her hands shaking, she quickly tried to open her cast iron gate. Glancing down she clumsily fumbled with the latch. When she looked up, Kim Park was standing on the other side of the gate. The vampire smiled ominously, her teeth ice white needles circled by black lipstick.

'You are such a sweet girl,' Kim said, straightening Rita's beret with a long fingernail. 'Tell me... pretty girl, is your friend clever?'

'I would say so,' Rita said, hoping her courage was about to return.

'Yes, I suppose you would say that. Word of advice for you... always be cautious when choosing your friends.'

'And why's that?'

'Because it's disappointing when they let you down.'

'Is that something you'd know all about?'

Kim did not reply but ran one finger down the side of Rita's face. The touch was cold, sharp, and painful.

'Tell your friend to let go of what he doesn't understand,' Kim said, her fangs gleaming within her twisted smile. 'If not, there will be no mercy for him and real trouble which he won't be able to fly away from.' With that said, she began to float into the air.

As she gently glided away into the night sky, her eyes never left Rita.

The effect on Rita was one of puzzlement but also genuine fear, and she felt a chill travel down her spine.

# CHAPTER TWENTY-FIVE

## Poison Pen

At six hundred and two Seneca Street, Lester Thyme once again rose from his bed. Yawning, he shuffled into his kitchen.

He then filled a silver percolator with water and opened a packet of aromatic Indian coffee. It was his second cup of coffee that morning, and he decided to make pancakes to go with it. His royal-blue kitchen, always a mess, was just about big enough to accommodate all the dirty pots and plates he had collected.

As the bitter smell of coffee and sweet maple syrup intertwined, Lester was certain he had heard someone knock on his front door. He rushed through the living room and into the yellow-tiled hall. By the time he opened the front door, there was no one there. Disappointed, he shut the door and made his way back to the kitchen. He failed to notice a small envelope that had been pushed through his letterbox. Instead, he was distracted by the thought of eating the soft pancakes and sipping sugary coffee.

After breakfast, Lester showered and chose a black tie to go with his white shirt. Putting on his bowler hat, he looked at himself in the mirror. The clothes he had bought were looser and he seemed to have lost weight. He also looked better, fresher, and more awake than usual.

As he prepared to leave the house, Lester finally noticed the envelope lying in the hall. He wondered if it was a letter of thanks from the museum. Maybe it was even fan mail? He decided he could do with cheering up and opened the red and silver envelope. From out of it fell a one-page letter with a distinctively pungent smell.

'Phew!' Lester exclaimed, and he covered his nose as he read the letter.

185

*Thursday, January 16th*

*Dear Mr Lester,*
*I would like to ask you, politely, to drop your current investigation. But I have decided not to and will issue the following threat:*

*Drop the case now! If you don't, then you will experience pain and suffering the likes of which you cannot imagine.*

*You are a bumbling fool, playing at being a super-cool sleuth and the activity does not suit you. You are nothing but an interfering loser, and you have been warned.*

*Your cards are marked!*

*Your new friend,*
*D.*
*P.S: I made a nice dragon curry once. Do not tempt me to repeat the recipe!*

Lester did not like the sound of the letter: it was both rude and threatening. He certainly did not like the idea of ending up in a curry.

'I think I'd better call Donnelly,' Lester said to

himself. 'Keeping him in the loop might keep me out of trouble.'

He picked up his telephone and called Inspector Donnelly. They agreed to meet at nine o'clock that night. He hoped they could get some information from the letter.

# CHAPTER TWENTY-SIX

## Voices in the Wind

Although all the children had gone home to bed, the fairground in Neon City stayed open until ten o'clock at night. The bright lights and smell of candy floss comforted Lester. The area was spick and span like always. The steep roller-coaster passed by, clanking and whooshing. Neon lights lit up a small sign above its entryway which promised the thrill of your life or your money back.

The night became colder. Lester tightened his coat around him and listened to a Miles Davis record which was coming from a cafe close by. A light mist was moving towards him. He looked down at his watch and realised Donnelly was ten minutes late. As he looked up, he saw the inspector appear from out of the mist.

'Going cold isn't it, Mr Lester?'

'It is with waiting for you. Where have you been?'

'Another day, another lot of burglaries.'

'Really?'

'Indeed. This city is becoming more light-fingered by the day. Where's your partner?'

'She's taking a day off.'

'A rest will do her good. You look a bit under the weather yourself. If you don't mind me saying so,' Donnelly said.

'No, I don't mind you saying so,' Lester replied, and he unfolded the threatening letter.

'Now then, what do we have here?' said the inspector, accepting the letter.

When Donnelly had finished reading the letter, he looked both surprised and worried. 'Are you afraid of heights?' he asked, then cupped his hands together and blew warm air into them.

'Me? No… heights are fine. Why do you ask?' Lester said and gulped.

'I'll tell you when we're higher up. Please follow me.'

Donnelly walked towards a slowly rotating Ferris wheel which whistled like an instrument of torture. At the entrance to the wheel, he bought two tickets so he and Lester were seated next to each other in a compartment. The wheel began to rock and shudder; it grunted and groaned as if coerced into its duties. Lester placed his hand on the rim of the open car. It was ice cold to the touch and he realised they would be colder when the Ferris wheel reached the top.

At one point, as their compartment climbed higher, the Ferris wheel made a metallic whine as if it were in pain. Lester looked around feeling nervous, but Donnelly had appeared calm and silent throughout the journey. He looked at his watch when their compartment reached the top. 'We've two minutes until the wheel moves again.'

'And I'll make the most of it. But couldn't we have discussed this over a milkshake in a cafe?'

'Up here,' Donnelly said, pointing a finger up to the sky, 'no one can hear us or read our lips.'

'Isn't that a bit paranoid?'

'Maybe, but I think we're both knee-deep in

something rotten: shop and museum burglaries, jewellery robbed at wand point, and now threatening letters? Are you confident this letter is for real?'

'It seems to be, and it was addressed to me. It makes its point crystal clear.'

'But what kind of an idiot puts his signature on a threatening letter?' Donnelly asked, shaking his head from side to side. 'I once knew someone who tried to steal this Ferris wheel. But obviously, he is not the stupidest person in Neon City. If this letter isn't a hoax, we now know their first name begins with the letter "D".'

'Does it?' Lester asked. 'Maybe "D" is the first letter of his or her surname?'

'That's a point. I…' The inspector stopped mid-sentence, then passed an angry look across to Lester. 'I hope you've not come here to accuse me of sending a letter like this to you?'

'Did you?'

'No. I certainly did not!'

'Then you've nothing to worry about, have you?'

'No, I don't suppose I do,' Donnelly said, and he leaned back in his seat to take another look at the letter. 'When did you receive this?'

'Sometime this morning.'

'It stinks terrible, but how do we catch the rotten hand that wrote it?'

'To begin with, I think it's safe to assume this is from whoever stole the antique swords and tried to steal the Jade Mask,' Lester said. 'And I want you to check the letter for any fingerprints. Other than mine or yours.'

'I'll do that. But I warn you to be on your guard from now on. You don't want to push your luck and fall from a great height.'

The Ferris wheel compartment rocked forwards due to a strong gust of wind; rusty metal parts screeched as they rubbed against each other. Lester looked over the side and down at the neon lights far below.

'Everyone seems to be warning me. All about a few old swords.'

'There is something more,' Donnelly said.

'What's that?'

'Call it a hunch. Are you familiar with the name Ermington Snyde?'

'Doesn't ring any bells. You think this Snyde character has something to do with this?'

'He was still in prison when all this started,'

Donnelly said, rubbing his chin. 'But since his release, things have gotten more out of hand. The crimes are getting bigger, the things taken more valuable. Seems like escalation to me. This Snyde fellow has a criminal history, but these items being stolen are diverse. Jewellery, power tools, construction equipment, weapons, and even clothing. It all seems unrelated but something tells me it's all connected. I just can't make the dots join together.'

'You've met this Snyde?'

'Certainly have. All brains and no feelings. He's a charmer but vicious with it. Not a man you want to trifle with if you can help it.'

Lester let the words sink in. He then considered what to do next. 'Any idea where he is?'

'No, he doesn't mix with low-level criminals. He's big time. Perhaps someone in the underworld may know his location. But I've no contacts in that circle of evil.'

'I might.'

'What!' Donnelly said, rising in his seat. 'How? You're not an ex-con are you?'

'Certainly not. But I assume you've heard of a man called Crafty Blue?'

'The King of the Underworld? Who hasn't?'

'He wasn't always so high up in the food chain. At one time we were honest business partners but then he went down the avenue of crime.'

'What makes you think he'll help? He could be involved in all of this.'

'No, not Crafty. I can't explain it, but it seems too complicated for him. He likes things nice and simple. He might not know where Snyde is, but he could know something about him. Crafty may decide to help me out of obligation. I lost every penny in one of his schemes, but he always liked me. Maybe he thinks he owes me.'

'That sounds promising. Do you need some backup?'

'No, better not. Crafty is like a wolf, he'll smell it coming a mile away.'

'If he's dangerous, are you up to the task?'

'Relax,' Lester said. 'I have renewed confidence in myself.'

Beneath them, the Ferris wheel rocked back into life. The steel within it began screaming.

# CHAPTER TWENTY-SEVEN

## Where the Pavement Ends

It was just like Crafty Blue to own a jazz club in the most overpriced part of Neon City, Lester thought. He stopped walking to unwrap a hard-boiled sweet known as a Fizz Ball. As he placed the sweet in his mouth, he continued walking and crossed a floodlit ashen grey bridge. He then followed a pavement that led away to a half-circle path. It was a leisurely walk and enjoyable because it took you away from the noise of the city. The path was sided by open fields decorated with trees of brown, gold, red, and yellow. There was a slight blue mist rolling over the grass fields.

Although no longer cold, Lester enjoyed deep breaths of the cool night air. They refreshed him and he felt the tension in his shoulders loosen. He liked being out in the night air. The night was exciting and unpredictable. It could lead you to dangerous places and people you would never ordinarily meet.

The waterfront area, which Crafty owned, was at the end of the path. Lester walked around the marina. He passed a thin moat of blue water and glanced at his large sapphire reflection. The liquid barrier surrounded an apartment block known as the Flood Building. Behind it was the Sonoma Jazz Club which connected to the waterfront. Outside the entrance to the club were five large doormen who were there to keep undesirables, such as the police, out.

Coming from inside the club could be heard the sweet and spicy sounds of a jazz band playing. Lester gave his name to one of the doormen who went inside to check with Crafty. The doorman returned and allowed him in.

As Lester walked in, he noticed a large gold cocktail bar thick with customers paying exorbitant prices for drinks. Throughout the club, there was harsh red lighting which seemed to fade in and out. Towards the middle of the club was a stage surrounded by tables and chairs. One table had the best view of the stage and was set out alone from the rest.

On the stage was a six-piece jazz band whose drum beat was erupting. The band looked on edge. As Lester watched them, he noticed they were focusing on the single table set out on its own. It was as if they were vying for the attention of a god, hoping to be in his good favour.

Instinctively, Lester walked over to the lonely table. Crafty Blue was sitting there and his table was overflowing with mince pies, crumpets, scones, and pots of jam.

Crafty looked up and initially said nothing. He was pushing a blackthorn walking stick from one hand to another. The silver falcon head atop the stick glinted under the lights.

'You look good,' Lester said.

Crafty Blue nodded and leaned back in his chair. He was a thin man with thick salt and pepper hair, and a moustache of the same colour. He was around six feet and dressed in a tweed suit. Outwardly he looked handsome and refined.

'It's good to see you, Lester,' he said, with a voice

that sounded like it had been pickled in hydraulic fluid. 'The night has been lonely to me; please keep me company.'

Lester seated himself at the table but moved slightly back as he saw Crafty's right hand slowly coming towards him.

'Please,' Crafty said. 'If only for the sake of appearance.'

The right hand was smooth and unlined. Lester noticed it was decorated with four black diamond rings. He shook the hand and saw a smile fleetingly dance across Crafty's face.

'You've done well for yourself,' Lester said.

'Business is brisk once the law has been paid off. I've no debts to think of either. Is that why you're here?'

'Relax, your taxes aren't due,' Lester replied, taking off his bowler hat and placing it on the table.

Crafty let out a deep mocking laugh. 'Please let me quench the thirst of honesty. What'll you have?'

'Coffee on the rocks.'

'Good,' Crafty said. He waved a waiter over to their table and said, 'Bring my friend here an iced coffee and a plum in an envelope.'

'You didn't need to do that,' Lester said.

'I owe you,' Crafty whispered. 'If you don't take it with you, I'll have to throw it in the trash.'

Lester sipped his coffee and put the envelope on the table. 'What do you want in return?' he asked.

'They say you like talking to policemen at the fairground.'

'Just a friend, Crafty. Just a friend.'

'But a useful one to have. Tell me, does he know who I am?'

'Everyone knows you.'

'That is true. Which makes me wonder why you spoke with him and why you now want to speak with me?'

'It's not about you. But it may be something you can help with.'

'And what would be in it for me?'

'It would put you back in my good graces. If I may be so bold?'

Crafty looked away from the table and towards the jazz band. He looked unimpressed.

'Which would mean,' Lester continued, 'that I would owe you a favour in return. When you need it.'

The band on stage began to quicken the pace. A saxophonist played one note and the drummer began to beat out a tense rhythm.

'Tempting,' Crafty said. 'And what is it that you want?'

'To know all about a character called Ermington Snyde, and where he might be.'

Crafty immediately turned in his chair and his face was now level with Lester's. His attention was rapt. 'Do you realise who you're asking about? That isn't an upstanding member of the community.'

'Understood,' Lester said, trying to act cool. 'Clue me up about him.'

'That cat is worse than an explosion and far more damaging. Do you get the drift I'm putting into your sails?'

'Let's not rock the boat just yet. We're only talking and I'm only asking a question.'

'A dangerous one at that.'

'You think I can't take him?'

The drummer was now pounding his drum kit like a maniac. His shirt was soaked with sweat, and his long black hair appeared wet near his forehead.

'Not in a million years,' Crafty replied. 'He's always

alert and you like to sleepwalk. He's ready to change the world at any time.'

'The world doesn't change often.'

'No, but when it does it tends to roll over anyone in the way. Particularly people like you. To survive in this city, you have to be hard and shifty. You are neither of either.'

'You sound worried about yourself.'

'I am. At the end of the day who am I? This club, or the property and money I have? No. When, and if, trouble breaks out those things won't help me at all.'

'What will?' Lester asked, genuinely surprised to see the fear in Crafty's face.

'Real friends. I have them in short supply as I spent my whole life ripping other people off. It made me rich. I never thought about it much. I just saw it as the law of the jungle, rules of the cage, or Social Darwinism. But that has isolated me and made me weak. Everyone who works for me is in it for themselves. Who am I to trust? What I should have done was to make more genuine and powerful friends. The kind who would look out for me, not the superficial. All I am now is a guy who hides in here and hopes to be forgotten about.'

'How about making some real friends in the outside world?'

'And how do I make those friends happy?'

'Tell them about Ermington Snyde,' Lester said, spreading strawberry jam on a scone. He took a bite of the syrupy jam and the scone crumbled in his mouth. Leaning back, he smiled and wondered if he would get an answer.

Crafty Blue held up his walking stick and looked at the falcon head.

'I have no idea where he is, but I can tell you where he's been. You want a story?' he said. 'Let me begin. Once upon a time in Malaysia and Singapore, there were many secret societies. Crime was their trade and profit. They all grew rich. But as a consequence, there were many conflicts. Those rowdy arguments became violent. For that reason, in 1889, Governor Sir Cecil Clementi Smith banned secret societies in Singapore.'

'What has all this to do with Ermington Snyde?' Lester asked.

'Be patient,' Crafty replied. 'Now, all those societies had a meeting. They all wanted to continue but realised they would have to tone down their act. They decided that all disputes would be solved with underground chess matches. One such player for hire was your friend Ermington Snyde. Nothing was known about him when he arrived at a Victorian dock known as Tanjong Pagar. But the man had skills which were in demand.'

'That's all a long time ago,' Lester said, his hands folding a napkin in front of him.

'Is it? The chess match idea never went away. They are still used to settle corporate disputes. All of which was fairly lucrative for Mr Snyde. He opened businesses and stockpiled cash. Until he lost it all.'

'What happened?'

Crafty turned to look at the band who were now improvising. He appeared, for a moment, to become engrossed in the music.

'Mr Snyde agreed to represent the House of Chang in a match, but it was a double cross. Someone higher up organised it. The result was a two-year prison sentence for Mr Snyde. And confiscation of all his assets, including a profitable chemical company. But that was irrelevant to a man of Mr Snyde's intellect. It was the loss of face that bothered him the most. If you're such a smart fellow, would you be happy about someone getting one over on you?'

'Who was higher up that organised the match?'

'I don't know. But either way… I wouldn't want to be in the Baron's shoes for all the tea in Assam.'

The band was now playing wild notes. A trumpet vibrated like a choked distress signal. The sound was abrasive and irritating to Lester.

'Why can't people just play straight?' he asked.

'Because they get bored of playing the notes in the same order,' Crafty replied.

'Play me one last song.'

'What's the tune?'

Lester took a pen from his pocket. He wrote a name and instructions on the envelope. 'Get one of your contacts to take care of this plum. Here's where I want it to go.'

'You won't change your mind about that?' Crafty asked, taking the envelope. 'One hundred thousand pounds is a lot of money. This could put you back on top.'

'I'm already back on top.'

'Don't be too quick to decide,' Crafty warned. 'Middle-aged guys like us should go slow.'

'Some of us can't afford to slow down,' Lester replied. He picked up his hat, nodded at Crafty and left. He followed a dark blue path at the rear of the club. It led him through a crimson orchard. The apples there were covered with a sheen from the night's chill. The dark fruit glistened like hot coals in the night. Behind Lester, the ivory moon looked on and carefully watched his back.

# CHAPTER TWENTY-EIGHT

## A Dangerous Profession

Rita Wong snuggled up in an oversized beige winter jacket in the chilly wind of a bright morning. A thin stream of smoke surrounded her. It was coming from a large pile of burning leaves; the smell was earthy, heady, and not unpleasant. She was sitting on a park bench watching a grey-haired old man removing brown leaves from the grass. He had brought a rake with him, and he moved back and forth dragging it slowly against the ground.

The small park was quiet and buffeted the sound of vehicles honking in nearby traffic. The peace was suddenly interrupted by a croaking call, similar to a mocking laugh, coming from above.

An unkindness of ravens was slowly circling in the honey-topaz sky. They landed just to Rita's left and approached looking for food. They had fattened themselves the day before with leftover fish and chips on Morecambe Bay. Now they were looking for a hearty breakfast. Three of them soon left, but one remained. He could smell something strong but could not decide if it was worth eating. Eventually, he got bored and decided to leave. Rita was sure she had heard him say 'Dragged through copper' before he flew away.

'Aren't you going to help that man with the leaves?'

Rita immediately jumped up at the voice coming from behind her.

'Lester, don't sneak up on me! You scared me to death.'

'You're irritable this morning. What's wrong?'

'Nothing. I'm just getting some fresh air.'

Lester held out a plastic tub that was full of bright yellow pineapple chunks. 'Want some?' he asked, opening the lid with a pop.

'Maybe later. Where have you been?'

'To tell the truth, I've become a bit of a nighthawk. I...'

'Yes?'

'What is that smell?'

'It's garlic.'

'Have you been eating Italian food?'

'No,' Rita said, unzipping her coat to show Lester a necklace she had made out of garlic. 'This is what I wear to keep away the undead.'

'Oh dear, does this undead have a name?'

'Kim Park. That vampire at the Jobcentre. The one who never stops whinging.'

'What? Kim "negative vibes" Park has been bothering you? What for?'

'She said she wants you to quit the case,' Rita replied, quickly zipping up her coat and adjusting her beret.

'I wonder what on earth she has to do with all of this. It can't have been pleasant to have been threatened.'

'I was scared at first. But now I'm angry. I've got two bottles of holy water in my backpack. If she threatens me again, I'll give her a shampoo and set she'll never forget.'

'You're not the only one who's been warned off. Yesterday I received a threatening letter.'

'Who sent it?'

'Someone with a first or second name beginning with the letter "D",' Lester said. He then went on to tell Rita about the letter plus his meetings with Donnelly and Crafty Blue.

'I think "D" is for Donnelly,' Rita said, and she helped herself to a sweet pineapple chunk.

'No, he's a policeman. Besides, what would be in it for him?'

'Maybe a retirement fund. He just seems a bit too clueless for me. Has he actually arrested anyone for these burglaries? Plus, he has a forensics team, and they haven't come up with anything either.'

'He could just be a bit stupid.'

'Even the stupid get lucky now and again,' Rita said, and she giggled as she looked at Lester.

'Yes, I suppose they do,' he replied and smiled. He then paused and his face became serious. 'If you'd told me six months ago I'd be in a game of life or death,' he added, 'I'd never have believed you.'

'I suppose we are gambling with our lives,' Rita

acknowledged. 'So what should we do about it, Kojak?'

'Who's Kojak?'

'He's a bald detective my dad watches on television. He—'

'Do you mind!' Lester said. He had become sensitive about losing his hair over the years. 'Don't let the Baldness Acceptance Movement hear you say that.'

'I'll try not to mention it again, but I think you need to toughen up.'

'Yes, I suppose I do. To recap,' he said, changing the subject, 'we have a considerable amount of stolen property. But no idea why it's gone or where it's going to.'

'Do people always steal where you're from?'

'They didn't use to, but things have got tough since the crash.'

'Crash?'

'Yep, financial crash. It happened shortly after prohibition.'

'What's prohibition?'

'Our people were becoming lonely and isolated.

The government said people weren't talking to each other enough, and technology got the blame. Computers, smartphones, and other items were banned.'

'No way!'

'Unfortunately yes way. I used to love spending hours on social media, but they had all that stopped.'

'My mum doesn't like it either,' Rita said. 'She thinks it makes people envious and jealous.'

'Well… I suppose that's true,' Lester admitted. 'But isn't all that part of being in a community? Anyway, since prohibition, all the technology companies collapsed. A lot of jobs were lost. Especially in mining, and the chemical industry. Living keeps getting more expensive but we all have less money. That's when theft became popular again.'

'Can't the government help?'

'They're short of money too.'

The old man had taken a break and was drinking coffee from a red Thermos flask.

Lester leaned back on the bench. He looked across the park into the large branches of an oak tree, which still had its red leaves intact. 'Everything will work itself out in the end. It's all about having patience,' he said and pointed to the old man. 'When he's cleared all those leaves, more will grow back and he'll be removing them again next winter. Everything works in cycles.'

'You're right, I should help him,' Rita replied.

'Yes. It will give you a break from our dangerous lives as detectives. Plus, the leaves are bad for the grass.'

# CHAPTER TWENTY-NINE

## Three Strangers

The hammering stopped at six o'clock at night. That was because Marvin, considering himself to be the leader, wanted a cup of coffee and a cream cheese bagel.

'Right, enough for now. Leave the floor tiles for a while. We're having a break,' he said.

Marvin's two companions dutifully dropped their tools and walked towards him.

A thick layer of dust drifted through the air in the high beams of a platform of white floodlights. Marvin had seated himself on the lower section; a plank of wood held his small feet above the ground. From out of his pocket he removed a cloth and wiped his long face with it. Then he unhooked his heavy tool belt and ran a hand through his white bone-straight hair.

'This job has dragged on,' Kitty said, draining an ice-cold bottle of lemonade.

'It's dragging on,' Marvin said, 'because I want it done properly. We're not cowboy builders. We're getting paid a lot of money for this job.'

'But do we even know what this place is going to be? Once the floor is in, then what do we do?' she asked.

'We're nearly done,' Marvin replied. 'Once we put the floor in, we just assemble the mechanism.'

'What mechanism?'

'That's not something you need to worry about,' he answered, his eyes narrowing with suspicion.

'But why us for this job? Why not get five trolls to do it. Why a bunch of humans?' Kitty asked, folding her arms in front of her.

'Because it will be harder to track us,' Marvin replied. Coarse grey dust fell from his hands as he wiped them with a cloth.

'I heard the police have our fingerprints from the burglaries,' Kitty said and bit her lip.

'They don't have our identities on file here in Neon City. And our fingerprints will be useless to them. Once we have this place done, we store all the stuff here. We should be done and ready to go in the next few hours.'

'You think it'll be that easy to walk away?' Kitty asked. 'I think you've forgotten who we're working for.'

# CHAPTER THIRTY

## Between Midnight and Dawn

The late nights had finally taken their toll on Lester. He had been sleeping more than usual. His dreams had changed from ones where he was falling to dreams of being alone. In the middle of one dream, he began to hear a telephone ringing. Through a wet and foggy street, he ran after the sound.

When Lester awoke, it was his home phone which was ringing. He looked at his clock, noticing it was Saturday and half-past one in the morning. Putting his dressing gown on, he made his way into the living room. On the way there he tripped over a stack of magazines and junk food cartons.

'I really must tidy up this dump,' he said, wondering why he hadn't cleaned up before.

When he got round to picking up the phone, it did not take long to realise who the caller was.

'You took your sweet time didn't you?!' the distinctive voice of Inspector Donnelly said.

'Do you realise what time it is?'

'A good detective never sleeps. Besides, I want you to come and meet me at the East Docks immediately.'

'Why?'

'It appears someone has been murdered. I need you here now and make it snappy!' Donnelly barked, before slamming the phone down.

Lester put his phone down gently and walked into the bathroom. Turning the cold water tap on full, he splashed some water on his face to wake himself up. At two o'clock in the morning, he dressed in black trousers, black shoes, and his trench coat.

When he opened the door, he saw it was foggy outside and raining heavily. He hesitated.

'Should I take it?' he asked himself.

'Better to have it and not need it, rather than the other way around,' Lester said. He opened a cupboard door in the hallway and took out a small cloth bag which he put into his inside coat pocket.

As he closed the door behind him, Lester looked up into the night sky.

'Two o'clock in the morning and raining,' he said, pulling his coat together and adjusting his bowler hat. He felt like he was in a scene from an old movie. The shadows of the night absorbed him. There was an icy wind blowing through Neon City and the temperature was about to plummet. It would be as cold as death.

# CHAPTER THIRTY-ONE

## The Drowning Pool

Reaching the East Docks, Lester prepared himself for the bad news. Inspector Donnelly was busy writing in his notepad. In front of him, two frog men were bobbing up and down in the dock looking for clues. Their splashes left ripples in the dark menacing water, which gave off an odour of pollution and fish. In the background, a generator hummed and powered a series of temporary lights.

'What's happened?' Lester said to Donnelly.

'We had a call that a body was seen floating in the dock. We arrived an hour ago and dragged the body out.'

'Have you identified it?'

'We have,' Donnelly said, his face a grim messenger of death. 'It's Baron Chang.'

'What?'

'I'm afraid so. I've asked a few officers to search the area for clues.'

'You're convinced it was murder?'

'The Baron couldn't swim, so I can't see him deciding to jump in for a few laps. We've yet to establish a time of death. But we can be bold and say this wasn't an accident. I imagine his lungs are full of seawater right now. This wasn't a mugging as he still has a wallet full of cash. And a fancy diamond watch on his wrist.'

'When I last saw him he was nervous.'

'Maybe he had good reason to be. Nevertheless, I have a suspect in mind already.'

'Who's that?'

'Atkins.'

'Walter Atkins?' Lester replied in disbelief. 'No, I don't think he had anything to do with this. He's no murderer.'

'He's aggressive when he wants to be,' Donnelly said. 'He certainly didn't have the Baron on his

Christmas card list. There's no telling what he might be capable of. People who are easily irritated are often the ones you have to be careful around. If the Baron hadn't slurred his character, Mr Atkins may have been more forgiving.'

'But what about Ermington Snyde? From what Crafty Blue said—'

'Come on, Mr Lester!' Donnelly said, 'Crafty ripped you off and left you broke. He's not known for his honesty. Everything he told you could just be a lie to waste your time.'

'No, I don't buy that. And what of the threats to Rita from Kim Park? Surely she has something to do with the thefts? I wonder about you, Donnelly. You've done nothing about Rita being threatened. Are you—'

'Now you listen here!' Donnelly shouted. 'I'm not the leader of some simple ragtime band! Kim Park walked out of the Jobcentre and they have no idea where she is. She's not been at work for three days. Don't you worry about her. No one threatens anyone on my watch. I'll catch up to her.'

'But I don't know why you would think Atkins committed a murder,' Lester said. Feeling exasperated with Donnelly's thinking, he decided to cut his losses. 'I'll check the Baron's mansion and tell Delilah Chang the bad news.'

'That's good of you to do so.'

'Check the Baron's wristwatch. There's a chance it's not waterproof. That should give you the time of death. He also carried a gold stopwatch; he couldn't have a conversation without it.'

'Good thinking,' Donnelly said, putting his notepad away. 'I'll tell my team to keep an eye out for it. In the meantime, I'm going to arrest Mr Walter Atkins on suspicion of murder.'

'He's not the one.'

'Do you know something I don't?'

'Nothing I could call real evidence.'

'That's of no help. But if your theory about the wristwatch is correct, perhaps Atkins has an alibi to keep him in the clear.'

'I certainly hope he does,' Lester replied.

# CHAPTER THIRTY-TWO

## The Friends of Baron Chang

When Lester arrived, he was surprised to see the gates at Priceless House had been left open overnight. No lights appeared to be on in the mansion either. He approached the elaborate decorations on the front door and knocked twice. There was no answer, and he continued to strike the door for two minutes. If anyone was in the mansion, they were not keen on guests.

Lester refused to believe Delilah was not answering on purpose. She didn't seem the type, and she certainly wouldn't hide from anyone. He was growing increasingly concerned for her safety as the minutes passed by. He decided the only course of action was to try to break into the mansion. From his previous visit, he knew the front door had three locks and was around four inches thick. He decided to see if the back door was less impenetrable. When he got there, it seemed the gold door was already open. He peered inside and saw a large kitchen.

Stepping inside, he closed the door behind him. The kitchen had a thick green carpet and heavy blue velvet curtains. A large sandalwood countertop occupied the left-hand side of the room. The kitchen was big enough to also have a dining table, armchairs, and a television.

Looking through the kitchen cupboards and drawers, Lester found no evidence of any use. However, he was struck by how well-stocked with food the kitchen seemed to be. Cupboards were full to the brim with cereals, chocolate bars, crisps, and tinned foods. He checked the refrigerator. Again, it was also full of food including deep-filled mince pies, pasties, doughnuts, pizza, and a large supply of milk. He picked out a smooth cold jar to take a closer look at it. The label stated it was full of Beluga caviar.

The amount of food perplexed Lester. Only the Baron and his daughter lived at the mansion. Delilah seemed so thin that Lester wondered if she ate anything at all. It was fair to say the Baron was plump, but even he couldn't eat such a large selection.

In the living room, Lester found four wood and canvas armchairs assembled around a projector screen. Scattered around the room were piles of fast-food wrappers and milkshake cups.

'Looks a bit like my house,' he said to himself.

In one corner of the room, there was a gold post-tray perched on top of a white marble table. It contained a collection of the Baron's letters, and Lester began to look through them. A large amount of the mail consisted of letters offering credit cards and cosmetic items.

On a writing table in the corner, he found a letter written in distinctive handwriting which had been signed by Ermington Snyde.

'It has today's date on it,' Lester said, and he looked behind him to see if he was being watched. Across the room was a large window with purple silk curtains rustling in the cold breeze. Deciding there was no one there, he continued to read the letter.

*Saturday, January 18th*

*Dear D,*
*The day comes forth, and I ask if you are now ready for the task which must be fulfilled.*

*I have considered the price you asked for supplying an army. I am happy to tell you that I accept. Upon delivery of the full army, I shall pay you the five hundred million yen you require.*

*I ask that you allow me one month to convert my gains into cash. I hope that my previous payments to you have inspired confidence.*

*I look forward to seeing you. Write to me soon and confirm your place in history.*

*Yours sincerely,*
*Ermington Snyde*

Lester gasped in shock. The Baron had been letting Ermington Snyde stay at Priceless House? If he had, did Delilah know? Was she in on it too? Was she the "D" mentioned in the letters?

Deciding not to pass judgement too quickly, he decided to look around other areas of the mansion for more evidence. As he walked out of the living room, a small brass door built into the wooden staircase in the hall caught his eye. It had no handle, just a circular red and black dartboard in the centre.

'Very strange,' he mused.

Lester approached the door and put Ermington Snyde's letter in his back pocket. With both of his hands, he pushed against the door several times, but it would not move an inch. Then he tried to pull the dartboard off the brass door, but there was no chance of it moving either. To the left side of the brass door was a small painting in a gilt frame. It was a picture of three bulls grazing in a field. A small farmer was standing near the bulls, pointing at his chest to indicate himself.

'Honestly,' Lester said. 'Modern art.' It then occurred to him that he had missed something. 'I get it. Bulls and I, *bull's eye*!'

He pushed the red circle in the middle of the dartboard. A loud metallic click pulsated through the air. The brass door opened.

Just through the door, a set of dusty blue painted

steps led down to a basement. Lester took one step at a time and slowly navigated the secret staircase. 'I wasn't made for these narrow paths,' he said quietly to himself.

The basement seemed enormous. It had a putrid musky smell. He felt around for a light switch and found one.

Floodlights lit up the room. It appeared to be the size of a warehouse and was packed with what looked like stolen items.

In one corner, he found all sixteen of Mr Que's swords. The black samurai swords were arranged in a neat row. Their gemstones glittered under the light, and he noticed the handles were wrapped in purple silk. Up against the walls, there were also several pieces of antique furniture. He was willing to bet they all belonged to Mr Atkins. On top of them were the stolen VIP rings.

'That'll be a weight off Donnelly's mind,' Lester said to himself.

That was just the tip of the iceberg. There were hundreds of bottled potions packed into brown cardboard boxes. Across from them were several power tools piled up. A nearby table was stacked with weapons of one kind or another. The strangest thing was the thousands of outfits piled against one wall of the room. They appeared to be red military uniforms.

'Uniforms for soldiers but with no soldiers in them,' Lester said to himself. 'And where are the thieves who stole them?'

Looking over his shoulder, Lester spotted a desk with a telephone on it. The red telephone was under a large clear plexiglass cover. 'I suppose now is a good time to contact Donnelly,' he thought. Taking a seat, he lifted the cover and dialled Donnelly's phone number. The line rang out and, while waiting, Lester removed Snyde's letter from his pocket to reread it.

He was certain that he had seen the letter "D" as a name shorthand somewhere before. Perhaps Rita was right. Donnelly could be the one arranging the army. He had more than enough officers within easy reach. It was possible he had yielded to temptation and joined the bad guys. The proof was all in a signature he had seen before, but where?

'My wallet!' Lester said, putting his hand into his coat pocket.

'Damn! I must have left it at—'

He sat still as a strange and dull pain spread across

the back of his head. He looked down and thought he saw the leaves of a hawthorn tree at his feet. He fell off the chair and landed face down into the leaves. Inch by inch they consumed him until his consciousness had been buried within them.

'That ought to keep him out of your hair for a while,' Kitty said , putting the monkey wrench back in her pocket. She pulled her long blonde hair into a ponytail and fixed it into place with a rubber band. 'Look at the size of him, how are we going to—'

'Stop complaining. Just pick him up,' Ermington Snyde ordered.

# CHAPTER THIRTY-THREE

## Phantom

The streets were full of clowns and police officers. The buildings around them twisted and leaned over in bizarre angles. They almost looked as if they had been cut from paper by a child. From a dark and tilted alleyway, Lester Thyme emerged into the sunlight. At his feet, his shadow seemed slick and glistening. Bending down, he ran his hand over the ground. It appeared his shadow was made of black paint.

'Strange… and the paint is still wet?' Lester said to himself.

The shadow was not the only painted object in

sight. As Lester walked around the surrounding streets, he discovered that the green cypress trees and yellow buttercup flowers were merely paintings on huge canvases. At the side of him, a damaged light was flickering. Upon closer inspection, the glow of the streetlight was also revealed to be composed of white oil paint.

Lester jumped and turned around at the sound of a train whistling. Behind him, there was nothing there except a clown in a red wig with a bemused expression on his face.

'Begging your pardon,' Lester said.

'Not to worry,' the clown replied in a metallic voice. 'Would you like to buy some roller skates?'

'No, I've really no use for them,' Lester answered and looked at a pair of blood red boots the clown was holding out.

'But you'll miss your train,' the clown said, scratching his red plastic nose.

'Which train?'

The clown rolled his blue eyes and said: 'Better take them. Otherwise, you'll be in danger… of missing your appointment.'

'No, really I—' Lester was interrupted by a popping

sound, and a flash of blue light. As he looked down he noticed the roller skates were now on his feet. They were also beginning to roll down a steep incline and they were taking Lester with them.

'Whoa! Please help me,' Lester shouted. The people around him stopped to stare but did nothing.

From behind him, Lester began to hear police sirens. 'Honestly, can this get any worse?' he asked himself as the roller skates continued to pick up speed. Yet he began to relax as his journey seemed to be taking an awfully long time. He began to examine his surroundings. On his right, a succession of mirrors lined the fronts of several buildings. Lester looked at them and noticed his appearance was distorted. 'I looked thinner in that last mirror,' he said to himself, 'things could be worse.'

Turning to his left, Lester saw a gigantic busy market. Under its vast red and green tarpaulin, it was thronging with people. Many of them were lined up at colourful food stalls. Lester saw an array of dishes including gooey chocolate cakes, spicy sausages frying in olive oil, and freshly baked garlic breads. He also saw Donnelly leaning against a lampost and eating a hamburger.

'Donnelly, I need some help here!' Lester shouted out, but the inspector ignored him.

The roller skates began to glide ever faster over the streets. They were taking Lester out of the city and into a small village coated in greenery. He noticed that the landscape was becoming more bizarre. The leaves on the brown topaz trees were jagged and the emerald grass was sharp like scissors. Ahead of him was a large red and green pool of water. The liquid in it was dirty and muddy, the surface of it violently disturbed.

'Oh no, I'm not going in there,' Lester thought, and he leaned back as far as he could. The roller skates made a grating noise but they began to slow down. They stopped just at the edge of the pool, and Lester felt a sense of relief. He collapsed onto a small patch of painted grass to try and get his breath back. His joy was short-lived. From above he heard a series of clicking sounds followed by the loud ring of a bell.

'What is that noise?' Lester asked aloud. As he looked up he saw a humongous yellow staircase coming from the heavens. It was covered with calcium white spikes and coiled like a snake about to bite. A figure clad in black was descending the staircase. Her

coal black hair hung down to her shoulders and she stared at Lester with a look of pure hatred.

'Whatever she's selling,' Lester mumbled, 'I bet it doesn't come with a refund.' He decided his best plan of action was to get away and he tried to stand up straight. The woman was descending the staircase more quickly, and getting closer to him in the process.

'Oh, come on,' Lester grumbled as he wobbled on the roller skates and nearly fell over.

The tall woman in black had removed a wand made of bone from her pocket. She was beginning to aim it at the dragon.

Lester got ready to be hit. As he did, there was a slight tap on his shoulder.

'Time to wake up, pretty boy,' a voice behind him said.

As Lester turned around he saw a small monkey dressed in oversized red silk trousers smiling at him. It then threw a large bucket of green tea all over him. Lester thought he could smell juniper and then everything went black.

# CHAPTER THIRTY-FOUR

## House of Games

As Lester Thyme moved his head from side to side shaking himself awake, he realised he had been dreaming. However, there was a cold liquid all over him. Ermington Snyde was standing over him and leering. He looked both angry and amused. In his right hand, he was clutching an empty pot. He had thrown the contents, cold oily coffee, all over Lester.

'Can you give me your address for my laundry bill?' Lester said, genuinely annoyed that all his clothes now stank of days-old coffee.

'I'm afraid not. But your hat is still nice and clean,' Ermington said, putting the black bowler hat on

Lester's head. He straightened his top hat and said: 'You're not one of us. So may I ask why you are here?'

'I could answer that if I knew where I was,' Lester replied, taking a quick look around, and realising he was still in the secret basement. He was also sitting upright in a wooden chair to which his legs were tied with rope. In his lap, he could see his hands were now encased in large metal handcuffs.

Lester been placed in an elaborate metal cell, shaped like a box. On each side, there were four metal bars with one side including a door. The cell bars were close together, and he realised squeezing himself through them would be impossible. The bars were also welded to a steel plate under his chair.

'Well, this is a nice prison you've built for me,' he said.

'I'm glad you're satisfied with your accommodation,' Ermington replied.

Lester wondered how long he had been unconscious, and checked his wristwatch. It read half four in the morning. Then, something more important crossed his mind.

'Where is she?' he asked, sluggishly.

'Who?' Ermington asked.

'Delilah,' Lester said, shaking his head from side to side and trying to correct his vision. 'What have you done with her?'

'This may sound like a cliché, but you should be more concerned about yourself.'

'Do I have something to worry about?'

'We all have things to be worried about. Baron Chang could have told you that. Now, why exactly have you come here?'

'Justice called.'

'You're a good liar. You didn't come here for justice. Interest in that debutante brought you here.'

'Debutante?'

'Miss Delilah Chang. Do you think she's even remotely interested in you? A person with no wealth or status. I think you waste your time on her.'

'She's a friend.'

'That's two lies,' Ermington said, winking.

'More importantly, why are you here?' Lester asked.

'I have big ambitions therefore I needed a bigger house.'

'I doubt you were invited. You know, if you're arrested again that will make you a two-time loser.

A second arrest could result in a long prison sentence for you.'

'But no one will know I am here or what I am up to. In twenty minutes you won't be breathing, let alone telling tales about me.'

'If you carry on talking like that, you'll never see daylight again. Can you at least tell me what this is all about?' asked Lester.

'I don't see why not. I have no objections,' Ermington said, stepping out of the cell. He then slunk his slender head between two bars and looked in at Lester. 'It's all about power,' he said. 'It always is. Over the years I've looked at Neon City and felt frustrated. As if I could run it better than the idiots in charge now. This city is in a mess and directionless. It was better in the days of the Greeks and Romans.'

'This city has never been perfect.'

'Yes, that is true. But the rulers want to search our homes now to know our thoughts. Then they examine our words for something they can be offended about and ostracise us for. The people know that and they're sick and tired of it. Change must come. Old powers should be thrown over and the slate wiped clean.'

'And you can do that?'

'I intend to.'

'I think you're deluded. The first sign of which is believing you can change the world all by yourself.'

'And the second?'

'Believing the world should be exactly how you see it.'

'I should have known a loser like you wouldn't understand.'

Lester gritted his teeth. 'I'm not a loser.'

'Yes, you are. You enjoy the company of other losers too. That pint-sized urchin called Rita. She has a house that's falling apart, just like yours. An elegant little bat told me that.'

'It seems Kim Park is a friend of yours. They do say you're judged by the company you keep. And with a winning personality like yours, it's no wonder you ended up friendless and broke.'

'I think I've heard enough of you, fatty dragon.'

'You, filthy fat shamer!' Lester replied.

'You're quickly upset,' Ermington said. 'I dislike the easily offended. They usually have something to sell, most often themselves. Now let's get down to business, shall we?' he said, and pulled a gold stopwatch from his pocket. 'You recognise this? This is a dead man's timer.' And he began to swing the stopwatch around his finger. 'Just like you, he didn't realise he was running out of time so quickly.'

'You must be proud of yourself. Being a psychotic murderer.'

'Maybe. I killed a well-known businessman. His death will be reported in the newspapers, but yours won't. Any memory of you will end here tonight.'

'Are you confident of that? I've never been dead before,' Lester said, accepting the end was near but trying to keep his dignity.

'Nothing educates like experience,' Ermington replied, and his mouth turned up in a cruel smile. 'Maybe now you'll drop that fake poker face you've been bluffing with. Especially as I'm about to cash you out.'

'Well, polite indifference is expensive,' Lester said. 'But condescending smug grins come cheap.'

'You are self-righteous. But your kind of smugness should be practised alone, at home, where it won't offend others,' Ermington said, walking back into the cell and placing a metal clamp over his prisoner's mouth. 'That should give my ears a break,' he added, patting Lester on the shoulder. As he walked back out of the cell he turned, locked the cell door and nodded.

'I must confess,' Ermington said, 'that prohibition stopped everyone from listening to drivel served up by the likes of you. The kind who sit in their underpants at two in the morning, giving lectures on social media.' He then turned and shouted.

'Kitty, get Marvin and that other incompetent. We're leaving now, and there's one more job to do.'

A clicking noise grew louder, and Lester found himself rising into the air. The cell was being winched up on a crimson cord attached to the ceiling. It then slowed to a stop. He guessed he was now about twenty feet up from the ground.

'Now the vat,' Ermington commanded.

Down below him, Lester could see three humans pushing an enormous container of liquid. It was easily big enough to swallow the entire cell, with Lester in it, without any difficulty.

'Now hear this,' Ermington called up to Lester. 'There is a lock which suspends the cell to the cord on the ceiling. It has a timer, which has been set to thirteen minutes. Once the timer is up, the lock will be released and the cell will go into the vat.'

Lester looked down and noticed the vat contained a clear liquid. He could see small bubbles rising to the surface. It looked dangerously sinister. The vat itself was silver, and its exterior was marked with lines of Sanskrit writing.

'He means business,' Lester thought. Above him, he could hear a clock ticking. It sounded like the heartbeat of a shark that had smelled warm blood in a cold ocean.

'Sayonara, Mr Thyme. And please don't forget to like us on Facebook,' Ermington said as he and his gang left.

Lester tried to reassure himself. There was a possibility he hadn't been searched and his bag was still in his coat pocket. 'I can make it out of this alive,' he thought, 'but I must be calm. Now where do I begin?' he asked himself. 'The handcuffs: I need to free my hands first.'

The heavy cold metal handcuffs had been firmly placed on Lester's wrists. He quickly realised he would not be able to slip his hands through them. They were far too tight.

Lester searched the library of his mind. He remembered a book by Houdini, the great escapologist.

Houdini had once said that handcuffs would open if you struck them hard enough against the keyhole. It was the only course of action Lester could take. He hit the handcuffs against the chair with as much force as he could muster. The chair vibrated as the handcuffs sprung open, and his hands were now free. He then untied the rope around his legs and stood up in the cell.

As he reached into his coat pocket, he was delighted to find his cloth bag still there. Inside it was a collection of lock-picking equipment including a pair of combination pliers, wire cutters, a piece of wire, and a small but powerful magnet.

Lester snipped the wire into two pieces and bent both up at the ends. He reached his hands around the cell door and tried to identify what lock was on the outside of the door. It felt like a Chubb lock. He then inserted both pieces of the wire into the lock. As he couldn't look at it face on, it would be a tricky task to open it. He began to twist and turn the wire, trying to catch the teeth to turn the lock chamber and open it.

After several minutes of twisting and turning the wire, Lester realised he was getting nowhere. He decided to try to adjust the wires. However, as he pulled his hands back in, he banged them against the bars and dropped both pieces of the wire.

What was he going to do now? All he had left were the pliers and his magnet. The magnet was strong, but it would never pick up the pieces of wire he had dropped.

'Hold on a second,' Lester considered, racking his brain. 'There's a Chubb lock on the outside of the cell door?' He realised the lock had only been turned once when Ermington locked it. It was a complicated lever lock but he could open it from inside the cell using a magnet!

Grabbing the magnet from on top of the chair, he placed it behind the lock and twisted it. The lock could be heard turning over, and then there was a loud click.

Lester pushed the door but it refused to move. He knew the lock was open, but the more he pushed the more obvious it became that he could not get out. By then it was too late. He heard the ticking clock stop, and a single chime ring out. The lock above sprang open. He grabbed the cell bars for support as the cage plummeted twenty feet into the vat. The cell quickly hit the bottom and was swallowed whole by the liquid.

Lester once again tried to push the cell door open. Then he realised his mistake and pulled the door instead, swinging it inwards. He left the cage and swam to the surface for air. As he climbed out of the vat, he removed the clamp from his mouth.

After searching the rest of the mansion for clues, Lester took a tram home. When he got there, he climbed into bed and hoped for a few hours of undisturbed sleep.

# CHAPTER THIRTY-FIVE

## The Harder they Fall

Lester steadied himself against the driving wind and rain. A dark sky above him seemed to have swallowed the sun whole. His emotions were anger mixed with expectations of finality.

Lester's path was blocked by a stagnant and dirty puddle of water. He waded through it without thinking. The streetlight reflections in the water were shattered and fell away.

A figure appeared out of the mist and rain. It stopped as it sighted Lester and placed a hand in its coat pocket. It paused for a moment as if readying itself for action. Then the figure set off running as fast as it could.

'Are you sure about this?' Inspector Donnelly asked, coming to a stop in front of Lester.

'More than sure. It was only a matter of time until I found out.'

Donnelly rubbed his chin. 'You know, once you start down this path there's no going back. Doing this could make you a lot of powerful enemies. You should consider your position.'

'You sound more worried than me.'

'Maybe. It's just all that's happened… it's—'

'Curious?'

'Yes. I suppose it is.'

'Everything has led to this,' Lester said.

'It is funny how things have worked out. But first, I should apologise for snapping at you the other night at the docks. I'm in a tricky position at the moment. I don't know who to trust.'

'How so?'

'Someone in the police force wants me out. Evidence has started to go missing. Witnesses have been changing their stories. Then they tried to bury me in paperwork.'

'Really?'

'Trust me. True villains always hide behind paperwork. All I can say is it's all been a bit stressful. Then all this nonsense. It's the strangest case I've ever known. The autopsy on the Baron revealed he drowned in—'

'Lemonade.'

'How in the world did you know that?'

'I've had a taste of it myself. I'll give you all the details later. For now, I think it's time you met the government employee mixed up in this racket.'

'Your phone call convinced me,' Donnelly said, removing a pair of handcuffs from his coat pocket. 'Then I did some digging myself. Enough for us to clean up Neon City, Mr Lester' he added, opening the door for both of them to step through.

'From now on just call me Lester.'

'My name's Bernard,' said Donnelly, holding out a hand.

'Good to know you, Bernard,' replied Lester, shaking the inspector's hand.

# CHAPTER THIRTY-SIX

## The Jobcentre Connection

Lester waited patiently in the queue. He had no appointment and was not expected. When the Warlock Devlin caught sight of him, he smiled like a piranha who had just detected someone drowning. He said:

'Come to sign on have you, loser?'

Lester nodded. Then he leaned closer to the grinning face of the warlock.

'Your signature is to prove your downfall.'

'How's that then, scrounger?'

Lester unfolded his Dragon Seeker's Allowance cheque and placed it on the warlock's desk.

'Mr Devlin,' he said, in a loud and confident manner. 'Is this your signature?'

'You know it is, you fool!' the warlock said, his face turning red with anger. 'You come in here to steal from the state every two weeks, and I give you a benefit cheque to do so.'

It was from behind the large figure of Lester that Donnelly emerged. He picked up the cheque and seemed convinced.

'Mr Devlin, I am placing you under arrest on suspicion of attempting to provide an army for a gentleman known as Ermington Snyde.'

'Nonsense!' the warlock said, and he pounded both of his fists onto the top of his desk. Around him, the room went silent. 'Where is your proof, you halfwits?'

'It's right here,' Donnelly replied, pulling two letters from his jacket pocket. 'The first item is a threatening letter to Lester with your signature on it. The second is a letter found at Priceless House, which you wrote to Mr Snyde accepting his initial payment. The signatures on the letters match yours. If that weren't enough, we checked with your bank. Mr Snyde has been depositing money into your account.'

The warlock's face flushed red with anger. His left hand started creeping towards his desk drawer.

'Ah, ah,' Lester said, and he reached over to shut the drawer. While Donnelly placed the warlock in handcuffs, Lester examined the contents of his desk. In a drawer, he found a spiky and vicious-looking magic wand. He pulled the stop cap to one end and emptied red dust from the chamber.

'Oh dear, oh dear,' Donnelly said, looking on. 'Possession of a dangerous and loaded weapon too. This isn't looking good for you. Maybe I should remove the handcuffs and wrap you up for Christmas? Now just where did you plan to get an army from?'

The warlock remained silent. Lester had been busily searching the desk and found a long paper list that gave the full explanation.

'He was going to get them from the Jobcentre,' he said.

'What? You can't put an advert in the window for an army.'

'My guess is that he was recruiting long term unemployed people who were desperate for the cash.'

'If that's the case, we can soon find out,' Donnelly said. 'I have all kinds of questions I want answering.'

'This also solves the recent spate of antique and jewellery thefts,' Lester said. 'Ermington was stealing them to raise money to pay Devlin for the army.'

'Where are the stolen goods then?'

'Tucked away in the basement of Priceless House, which is now the size of an airport terminal.'

'Seriously, when this lot shovel it, they use two hands don't they?' Donnelly picked up a phone from the warlock's desk and dialled a number. 'Jimmy, get some other officers and check out Priceless House,' Donnelly shouted into the phone. 'Keep an eye out for that Ermington Snyde character, and be careful.'

'You think this is all over?' the warlock said to Lester. 'You just watch your tail from now on.'

'That's enough of that,' Donnelly commanded. 'Come on, let's get you down to the police station,' he said, pushing the warlock in front of him. He frog-marched him across a dirty blue carpet, and through a haze of ozone gas coming from a photocopier.

Outside the Jobcentre, the sky had cleared and the sun was slowly creeping out. The damp air began to dry, and a rainbow appeared in the sky. Lester looked around Bush Street as if with new eyes. Somehow Neon City seemed friendlier, easier, and cleaner than before. He felt like a part of it, a needed part that was respected. His back straightened and his walk became more confident.

When Lester and Donnelly led their prisoner out of the Jobcentre, someone was waiting for them. The thief from the museum burglary stood outside with a golden bow and arrow. He was wearing his red satin cloak and the hood obscured his face. From behind, he was framed by the contents of an art and craft shop. A series of glass shelves crisscrossed, giving him the appearance of a murderous spider sitting in the middle of a glass web. A slick puddle of rainbow-coloured oil circled his feet.

Lester and Donnelly froze. Their prisoner was terrified.

'Where is he?' the hooded figure screeched. The question, like his arrow, was aimed at the warlock.

'Who?' the warlock asked, his body tensing and his shoulders pushing into his neck.

'Ermington Snyde,' the figure said, his voice becoming stronger and more metallic.

'I don't know!' the warlock pleaded, sweat dripping from his brow.

'I'll only ask you once more.'

'I believe him,' Lester shouted. 'And if I were you, I would put that bow and arrow down. If you kill him, you'll go to prison for a long time. You don't want a murder on your conscience.'

'He's right, son,' Donnelly said in agreement. 'If you put the bow and arrow down, we'll try to help you. Otherwise, you'll be in a lot of trouble.'

Silently the hooded figure considered his options. Then, he threw down the bow and arrow in defeat.

The warlock swiftly blew a sigh of relief.

Donnelly walked behind the figure and threw his hood back.

The eyes in Lester's head nearly popped out. Before him stood Delilah Chang.

'Delilah, I… where… how did you?'

'I was forced into helping with the burglaries,' she said. 'They forced my father and me to comply.'

'You were the mask thief?'

'It wasn't a career option,' Delilah said. 'They killed my father because he was going to tell all.' Her shoulders sank, and her beautiful face looked down at the ground. 'I didn't know what to do about it all. He was always like that. My father could never walk a straight line.'

'Regardless of that, I'll have to take you in for questioning, Miss,' Donnelly said.

'If you must,' she replied, taking a slight breath and looking up. 'Lester, would you call my lawyer?' she asked, passing a card to him. 'I'm sorry about everything. I hurt you more than—'

'That's not important now,' Lester said, smiling as he looked at her. 'It can all be put right. We better get started by calling your lawyer right away.'

# CHAPTER THIRTY-SEVEN

## A Better Tomorrow

When Lester arrived home, he began to prepare for a special event that would take place the next day. He began by tidying his house from top to bottom. Rubbish was cleared, plates were cleaned and the carpets were vacuumed. He put balloons up and wound out a large pink banner. He also piled several different kinds of food onto the kitchen table. He hung a string of red and green lights throughout his living room. From inside a large box, he removed an orange dance floor mat. There was then a guest list to write out and after that, he retired early to bed. It had been a long day indeed.

*　*　*

Rita shut the front door to her house and walked into the street. The house was now surrounded by scaffolding. There were hammering and clean snapping sounds in the air as roofing tiles were replaced. The following week all the bedrooms were to be plastered, painted, and carpeted. Her mother was currently engrossed in a catalogue, trying to pick out a new kitchen.

'Having some work done?' a voice behind her asked. As she turned around, Rita saw Lester standing with his arms crossed and smiling down at her.

'We are. Someone generously decided to pay off our mortgage. It's not a mistake either. The person who did it wants to remain anonymous.'

'Restores your faith in humanity doesn't it?'

Rita eyed Lester suspiciously. 'I don't think they were human, but they are good,' she said.

'Maybe they felt they owed you. Perhaps you helped put their life back on track?'

'Or maybe they just needed a slight push?'

'That is something you are good at.'

'So you say. You look different today?'

'Me? Ah… it's my hat. I left it at home by mistake. I'm going back to get it now. And to take you to meet some people who want to thank you.'

'Who's that?'

'It's a surprise. Come on, we don't want to be late.'

Lester gave Rita all the details of how the stolen swords case had been resolved. Then he revealed the fate of Delilah Chang, and how Warlock Devlin was now languishing behind bars.

When they arrived at the dragon's house, Lester passed the front door key to Rita.

'Who's inside?' she asked.

'Friends,' Lester answered. 'It seems we have plenty of friends now.'

A crowd of beaming faces greeted Rita when she opened the door.

'Happy birthday!' shouted the crowd in unison. They were framed by colourful lights, blue lanterns and purple tinsel. As Rita stepped inside, several party poppers were set off. A cloud of red and green paper confetti flew through the air, covering her and Lester from their heads to their toes.

'I have your first present right here,' Lester said,

brushing confetti off his coat. He then removed a blue-striped gift-wrapped box from his pocket and passed it to her.

'Thank you,' Rita said, quickly ripping the present open. Inside was a large pair of binoculars and engraved across both barrels was *Wong and Thyme: Private Detective Agency*.

'Thank you so much!' she said.

'You're more than welcome.'

'What's this?' Lester said, picking up a long pale-blue envelope off the hallway floor. On the reverse of it was a seal of red wax stamped with the image of a Merlion. He opened it. Inside was a small piece of paper which he unfolded:

*Sunday, January 19th*

*Dear Mr Thyme,*
*It seems I underestimated you, being as busy as I am, and I offer you my apologies. If we cannot accept responsibility for our own mistakes, then what good are we?*
*I write to you not as a peace offering but to advise you of the obvious. You are no*

*match for me or my aims. Through a mistake on my part, you have lived to tell the tale. But you may not be so lucky next time.*

*I, and my associates, will avoid you for the moment. If you insist on our paths crossing again, I assure you that neither you nor your partner will live to tell the tale.*

*Yours sincerely,*
*Ermington Snyde*
*P.S:* あなたのパートナーはあなたの健康を知っていますか？

'What is it?' Rita asked.

'Oh, it's nothing. Just junk mail,' Lester said and scrunched the letter into a ball.

Lester then led Rita to a large buffet on a wooden table in the living room. There was hot pizza, crisps, salted popcorn, sticky peanut butter sandwiches, bitter green tea chocolate, Chinese mooncakes filled with sweet red bean paste, and creamy rice pudding from Manipur.

Rita noticed Mr Que the goblin was chomping his way through a bitter chocolate and lime trifle.

'Did you only buy one trifle, Lester?' Mr Que asked.

'Yes. Perhaps that was a mistake.'

'I should say. What is everyone else going to have when… I say, are you wearing a wig?'

'No… I—'

'Yes, you are!' Mr Que said, his mouth now a wide grin. 'Look everybody, check it out. Bogey's got a syrup on!'

'Actually, if you must know,' Lester replied, trying to keep his temper in check. 'I've had a hair transplant.'

'Whoops, I made a mistake. It does make you look a bit younger though.'

'Really?'

'Yeah, by about six months.'

'So it is true,' Lester said, noticing the kitchen light shining off Mr Que's bald head, 'that jealousy often comes dressed up as criticism.'

The party went on all day and Rita was amazed by the number of people in the house. At one point she saw Donnelly walk out of the kitchen wearing a cooking apron. He was complaining that the custard tarts in the oven were burning.

'Did you not think to check the temperature?' Lester asked.

'I can't keep my eye on everything!' Donnelly protested.

At that moment, Mr Que discovered who the party's chef was, and he did not waste any time in making his complaints known. 'I should have known the police were involved in putting on such a substandard service. What on earth did you put in that green jelly? It's simply revolting.'

The look on Donnelly's face summed up his feelings and he stepped back into the hot kitchen. He was followed by Mr Que, who enjoyed dealing out further criticism for the remainder of the party.

Rita later learned that the Green Crane Museum had paid a reward for saving the Jade Mask. Also that Mr Que, as agreed, had paid a ten per cent amount for the retrieval of his swords.

'The director of the museum wants to thank you,' Lester said, pointing at a tall wizard in a grey pinstripe suit. 'Mr Aster, this is Rita Wong.'

'How simply splendid to meet you,' Mr Aster said, his silver eyes lighting up. 'I can't thank you enough,

Miss Wong. My museum would be simply ruined without your help. The Jade Mask has been a real crowd-puller since you helped foil the attempted theft of it.'

'Think nothing of it.'

'Well, I would but… that emerald ring,' he said, looking down at her right-hand index finger. 'Where did you get it from?'

'Oh, this? A friend lent it to me. Would you like to take a closer look at it?' She asked, about to remove the ring from her finger.

'Oh no! Please never take that ring off,' Mr Aster said. 'It's an original Vasuki. It allows humans to see our world. I doubt you would have ever seen Lester without it. Always keep it safe.'

'I promise I will.'

Mr Aster tried to say something more, but his words were drowned out by loud music now pumping throughout the house. To Lester's surprise, Inspector Donnelly seemed to be dominating the dance floor. He had placed a long furry pink scarf around his neck, and on his head was a gold trilby hat. Swinging his hips to *Abracadabra* by the Brown Eyed Girls, he waved his arms in the air. Then he folded them across his chest and lowered himself, moving his knees from side to side.

'Go for it, Donnelly!' Rita shouted.

'Get down and stay there,' Lester added, encouraging him.

'Yes, and don't ever get back up!' Mr Que shouted, his eyes narrowing and his mouth turning downwards.

As the party continued, Rita spoke to Lester in a quiet corner. 'Do we have enough money now to open our detective agency?' she asked.

'More than enough. We just need to find a vacant office in Neon City.'

'I can help you with that,' a voice said.

They both turned. Mr Atkins was smiling at them. 'I think this city is a lot safer with you two on the beat,' he said. 'And I might have a place that would suit you. I got myself into the property business recently. Why don't you try a room in my block, rent-free, for twelve months? I'll consider it a gratitude payment.' With that said, his hard face became smoother and his razor wire wrinkles softened.

'We won't say no to a favour from a friend,' Lester said. Both he and Rita then shook hands with Mr Atkins.

'Look,' Rita said. 'Over by the piano, it's Fritz.'

'Is that Chance Fosbery with him?' Mr Atkins asked, his amber eyes lighting up in excitement. 'It is him! That ghost is a graveyard poet. My word, you two keep good company,' he added, and dashed off to get a better look.

'I guess we are judged by the company we keep,' Lester said. He then nodded towards Fritz, who was sitting down to a baby piano in a corner of the room. Fritz swept a hand through his grey slicked back hair and adjusted the matchstick in his mouth. He looked back and nodded at Lester and Rita. At his side, Chance Fosbery tucked a red handkerchief into his pocket and lifted up a gold microphone.

'I think it's time this party was started,' said the large grey ghost, to a huge round of applause. As he began to sing, the emerald in Chance's front tooth twinkled like a star and his voice boomed like the sound barrier being broken:

> *Success is only a cobweb away,*
> *So pick yourself up and hear what I say,*
> *You've been filling in job applications,*
> *Begging to see some admiration,*

*Today the skies may seem awful grey,*
*But Tomorrow, success is a cobweb away.*

*You polished your résumé till it shines,*
*From the job market, you see no sign,*
*You're living at home, feeling alone,*
*The only friend for company is your phone,*
*But don't you worry, you can end this drought,*
*Open your front door and step right out,*
*Find a friend and start to make way,*
*Cause success is a cobweb away.*

*All you gotta do is accept a helping hand,*
*So swallow your pride and join the band,*
*You'll see more coin if you take responsibility,*
*And you'll soon impress with your adaptability,*
*I know it makes you feel delirious,*
*When they ask for years of experience,*
*But with or without them, you'll get to Broadway,*
*Because for you, success is a cobweb away!*

# CHAPTER THIRTY-EIGHT

## The Copper Lady

On a cold night, a small rusty train pulled up to a decayed concrete platform. The gently oiled brakes of the train sang with relief as it came to a halt. In one compartment, exhausted office workers shuffled out and began their journeys home.

When the train was empty, Ermington Snyde rose from his seat. Stepping out of the door, he looked around and shook his head at the colourless concrete and plain surroundings. Cheap fluorescent tube lights, placed on a high ceiling, removed any shadows and atmosphere. Posters littered a wall with dull efficient fonts designed to put readers to sleep. The overall feeling of the train stop was tiresome and flat. Walking past a small card shop, Ermington headed for the west of Neon City.

The air carried the scent of stale rain. Somewhere in the dark, a homeless wild cat hissed at a trespasser. It was a guardian of the dim alleys, foreboding streets and crowded bars lit by milky lighting.

Ermington ran his fingers over the smooth green painted iron of a set of gates. Welded to the top of the gate, ten feet off the ground, was a red metal number four.

'That will keep the superstitious out,' he said to himself. He gripped the gate and pushed it open. He was careful not to snag his new black suit on it. When he closed the gate, it pierced the air with a metallic screech.

Ermington began to walk along a black and white stone path partially covered by snow. Hanging chaotically over the path were the coppery-brown branches of birch trees. Ermington glanced at a gunmetal-black lantern flickering with blue flames. It crackled and then spat aquamarine embers onto the floor. Only the sight of a blue wildflower blooming in the snow raised his eyebrows. He continued his journey, elements of magic no longer making an impression.

Bricolage Tower, however, more than bothered Ermington. There was something about the forty-five-storey skyscraper that put the fear of God into him. The tower was grey, but it was an impersonal and inhuman grey. It was lifeless and uncaring.

Ermington stepped around a brick well. It was overgrown with thick green ivy and contained the dark slimy waters of the dead. From there, he walked into the ground floor of the tower. It appeared abandoned, but he knew that many eyes were watching him. He looked at the mosaic tiled floor, the pendulous trees, vast mirrors, and white pianos. The lobby's ceiling was held up by magnificent support columns decorated with sharp red logograms. There were flashes of light from Art Deco lamps. They cast enigmatic shadows and created an atmosphere of seductive decadence. An equally refined staircase led to a platinum lift.

'Criminality never advertises,' Ermington said under his breath. He looked at the elegant platinum lift with its red carpet, crystal walls, and thick gold buttons. Stepping inside, he reached for a large emerald button that had the number nine etched into it. He pressed the button, then the doors closed and the lift began its ascent while letting out a hydraulic purring noise. In the background, two gold speakers emitted music by Dimitri Shostakovich. Ermington recognised the piece but did not want to think about its subject matter.

While the lift headed up, Ermington considered his life's descent. He was over two hundred and fifty years old. He had worked hard all his life and where had it got him? Once again he was broke and abandoned. He had also spent more time in prison than the Count of Monte Cristo. Was that how life rewarded the determined? Now he was to go face to face with a woman who had bested him more times than he cared to remember. She was a model of success. Sitting comfortably in a tower built from the spoils of her criminal enterprise.

Bricolage Tower had been constructed from the most precious metals the earth had to offer. There were support beams of solid silver, rivets of gold, and floors of copper. Walls throughout the building were inlaid with pearls, rubies, and emeralds. The whites, reds, and greens sparkled in the beams of rhodium light fittings.

The whole building was like an open safe filled with the earth's minerals. Ermington wanted them all, and he hated the success they represented. He considered the building's owner to be an old scaly dragon. One obsessed with hoarding great wealth. Not so it could be used, but to prevent anyone else from having it. Her grasp for wealth was fuelled by the pleasure gained from making it elusive.

As the lift continued to rise, Ermington wondered if he would end up back on the streets. He then realised that was an option no longer available to him. He could never run away from Neon City. There could be no hiding in the real world, not while it was a place he no longer recognised.

The lift stopped and its doors clicked open. Ermington looked out to see a floor coated in dazzling diamonds. His black boots made contact but the surface did not give way. The room around them was thirty metres long, twenty wide, and hummed like a greedy incinerator. The light in the room was cold, blue, and creepy.

Above Ermington, a silver ceiling reflected his nervous walk. Ten feet ahead of him he saw a set of solid gold steps. They led to a copper-plated wall behind them, on both sides of which were large pale elder-wood bookcases. They were neatly lined with books, including some written by Marx, Orwell, and Wollstonecraft.

After four minutes of waiting, Ermington heard a clicking sound and then the ringing of a bell. He saw the outline of a small hand on the copper wall. Then the hand came through. It was pale white and flabby like a fish's belly. Its nails were sharp and painted black.

The copper wall began to emit clouds of deathly white vapour. Ermington lost sight of the hand but he felt his nerve endings ignite. The vapour travelled towards and through him. He was sure, at one point, he had felt an ice-cold hand grip his spine. He also felt a crippling loneliness as if all life around him had been removed. The room also felt tighter, almost restrictive. When the vapour disappeared, Ermington saw her enter the room.

Lady Malia Bricolage wore a black dress imprinted with a pattern of white reeds. In her right hand, she carried a wicker basket full of white chrysanthemums. Her hair was jet black and wispy; it was pulled away from her waxy forehead. Her facial features lacked definition. In her mouth were black razor-sharp teeth which had begun to crumble. They gave away her true age. She was an ancient ghost and a sinister one at that.

'Why, it's Mr Ermington Snyde. I did not know you were coming. I was just collecting flowers from my garden,' she said, one corner of her mouth turned up in a smile. Her face was one of pleasant surprise undercut with vicious aggression. She then walked down to Ermington ever so slowly, one step at a time, and her eyes sliced into him.

Ermington stood still and did not move. It was a poor attempt to project courage, and he knew immediately that she could smell his fear. His eyes narrowed, and his eyebrows lowered as he looked down at the floor.

'Have you brought back my ring, Mr Snyde?' she asked, her voice sounding like a saw cutting through bone in a butcher's shop.

'I am afraid I have not, Lady Bricolage. But I am still looking for it. In the meantime, I have put in place what you requested.'

'I see. Do they suspect anything?'

'No, of course not. You wanted a fool, and now you have one.'

'You were slow in arranging that. Never mind. You will now leave things as they are for at least two years.'

'What?' Ermington said, his fists clenching and forming balls. 'I ruined my plans for you. Now I have nothing to show for all my hard work, you can't expect me to—'

'When prohibition is repealed, I shall reward you.'

'You promised me retirement long ago, and long ago it was.'

'I am sorry, Mr Snyde. But you are not ready to go there... I wonder if you ever will be. Perhaps that is not a path for you.'

'If that is how you feel, I shall turn a deaf ear to you.'

'I think you have heard me clearly.'

'But it is a case of my honour.'

'When you were homeless in Lahore, Mr Snyde, did you have honour then? I seem to remember you were plucked from the streets by the British.'

'That was a long time ago.'

'It was, but you live in a perpetual childhood, Mr Snyde. One that is both destructive and also useless.'

'When I took the head of a detective, all those years ago, you did not belittle me so.'

'You merely corrected your error. Nothing more than that.'

'If you had any respect you would—'

'Silence,' Lady Bricolage commanded, and from behind her, several apparitions pushed through the copper wall. Ermington could see their egg-shaped faces had no eyes. They were covered in dust and cobwebs. Their teeth chattered like intoxicated vultures. He decided not to join their ranks and closed his mouth. The apparitions slowly sank back into the copper wall.

'Now,' Lady Bricolage said, holding a chrysanthemum in her left hand. 'I have many things for you to do.' She raised the gentle flower to her nose to inhale its earthy scent. 'I'd recommend you do my bidding. As you say, it is unpleasant to be without money. Is that not the case, Mr Snyde?'

Ermington removed his top hat and bowed deeply. His thick brown hair fell forwards and slightly out of place. 'What would you have me do?' he asked.

'Firstly, there is a corporation to deal with. It belongs to me, but the directors decided to load the business with debt. They then paid themselves large bonuses with the borrowed money.'

'Oldest trick in the book,' Ermington said, without surprise.

'Indeed. You will get my money back, and do the big job on them for me.'

'Accepted,' Ermington said, his eyes downcast. 'Is that all?'

'Not quite,' Lady Bricolage replied. 'I then want you to visit the Baldness Acceptance Movement.'

'The what?' Ermington said, his face upturned in a smile. He began to giggle.

'Yes, you heard me. Their far-left doctrine has cost one of my businesses a lot of money. Fred will give you the address for their headquarters. I want to speak to them personally. Understood?'

'Understood,' Ermington said and bowed trying not to laugh any more.

'Go now,' Lady Bricolage said, looking bored. 'But do not fail me,' she added and walked back to where she had come from. Behind her, a cloud of red smoke appeared and covered her as she disappeared into the copper wall.

'I will not fail,' Ermington said, hoping he was telling the truth. He then quickly marched away to the platinum lift. His body was hot and he felt drips of sweat run down his back.

# CHAPTER THIRTY-NINE

## Out of The Past

Tillotama Kumar turned up the heating in the *Sans Noir* coffee shop. So far, her business had endured one of the worst winters she could remember. At one point a frozen pipe had cracked and cost her a day's takings while it was repaired. Outside, the snow had become deeper and it hid a dangerous layer of ice. There were no small pools of water in the streets now, only treacherous sheets of transparent crystal.

A bell rang and a chilly draft passed through the empty coffee shop. The door had been opened wide, and Tilo was half relieved to have a customer. She heard the door gently close. 'Be right with you,' she shouted over her shoulder, still focusing her gaze on the central heating controls.

'Take your time,' a voice replied from the front of the coffee shop. Tilo recognised the voice but could not place it. 'Probably a regular I haven't seen for a while,' she mumbled to herself. Standing up, she walked onto the shop floor to take their order.

'You're still the jewel of Delhi,' Ermington Snyde said as Tilo stepped out of the kitchen. Her small figure was draped in a black striped dress, it rustled gently as she moved closer to him.

Ermington was sitting in a chair in front of the window. He was partially illuminated by sunlight and slashed by shadows made from the Venetian blinds. He was smiling, but Tilo thought he looked both disappointed and remorseful.

'It's been a while since anyone called me that,' she replied, placing her notepad and pen back in her pocket. She then walked over to the table and seated herself opposite him.

'You understand the trouble you're in?' Ermington asked her, placing the palm of his left hand on the smooth cherry-wood table.

'I thought you liked trouble,' she said and pulled

her thick glossy black hair back. She then applied a brown tiger eye clasp to hold her hair in place.

Ermington nodded his head and smiled. He placed his hands together in a steeple and looked across at her with eyes of friendship. 'I knew you had the ring,' he said. 'But I didn't want you to get into trouble or the friend of yours you gave it to.'

'Oh, you are such a tough cookie,' Tilo replied, her dark eyes mocking him. 'Do you honestly believe I care about anyone else anymore?'

'You think your heart is cold, don't you?' he said, shaking his head from side to side. 'I admit the past is a dark place,' Ermington said. 'But the sooner you move on from it, the faster you can move forward. Now... please don't make this a personal issue, Tillotama. I want that ring back within the week.'

'Or what?'

'Or life could become uncomfortable for both of us.'

'So?' she replied, crossing her arms across her chest. Her look of playful arrogance had been replaced with a look of stubbornness. She glanced at his eyes and then looked away.

'Suit yourself,' Ermington said, putting his top hat

back on his head. 'There are things outside of this world that you cannot win against,' he said. 'I always tried to protect you from that, but you think you can take on God and win. You need to realise that the world does not revolve around you.'

Tilo looked over Ermington's shoulder and glanced out of the front window. Among the falling snow, she saw an elderly Chinese lady standing by the road. She seemed to be talking to herself, then raised an arm in the air before setting off running along the pavement. It almost looked as if she was chasing someone or something.

Tilo stood up quickly. She clasped her hands in front of her, appearing almost needy. 'Please stay for coffee,' she said.

Ermington looked at her and then removed his hat. She lowered her head slightly, and her large brown eyes shone in the sunlight. 'Alright,' he said, leaning back in his chair. 'What do we do now?'

'You can wait,' she said. 'And I'll bring your favourite.'

# CHAPTER FORTY

## Destiny

On Continental Avenue in midtown Neon City stands a large brownstone building. On the eighth floor, room number eight-A has a large green door with a plate of glass in the top half. Etched on the glass with gold lettering reads *Wong and Thyme*.

Inside the office, Lester was reading a book by Raymond Chandler and Rita was calculating how much money they had spent on decorating.

It was easy to see where the money had gone. Both of them had a smart mahogany desk with a club chair. On both desks were vintage black telephones, and to the side were silver and chrome filing cabinets.

Rita had thought this was enough for the office, but Lester had insisted on purchasing a large glass mirror. His final touch was a green banker's lamp for each desk. He insisted the items would create a good first impression on new clients.

Lester leaned back in his chair. He flicked a small piece of dust from his grey wool suit before returning to his book.

'Is the story any good?' Rita asked.

'Complicated, but worth another read. All of his books are like that.'

'Good. Maybe you'll get the chance to read them all. I think we could use a break before our next case.'

'Don't get too comfortable,' Lester warned. 'This profession is unpredictable. Who knows what will happen in your next episode?'

Suddenly, the office door rattled and swung open. A large man entered who was sweating profusely. He began to dab his face with a green silk handkerchief. He had thick black oily hair, a pale complexion, and two large dimples on his Roman face.

'Are you alright?' Lester asked.

'Yes, I shall be in a minute,' the large man replied. He then helped himself to a glass of water from a cooler in the corner of the office. Once he had drunk the water with a loud gulp, he sat down opposite Lester.

'You are the famous private detectives whose names are all over the newspapers?' he asked.

'We are, and how may we help you?'

'I have an important case for you. Money is no object to a man like me. However, I need to be persuaded that you can handle a case as important as mine.' The large man eyed Lester suspiciously. 'I want no bunglers or fools who sleepwalk.'

Lester nodded and replied, 'We never sleep, and we can handle any case.'

'This is no ordinary case,' the large man said, and he once again dabbed sweat from his forehead. 'This is a case of mystery, magic, and circumstance. Come closer, I want to tell you all about it.'


The End

**Mark Jones** lives in the small village of Lowton near Warrington, Cheshire. He worked in Delhi for just under two years as an editor of graphic novels, and in Singapore for a little over a year as an English teacher. *Rita Wong and the Jade Mask* is his debut.